Begin your Moonlight journey today with a FREE copy of MOONLIGHT FALLS, the first novel in the Thriller and Shamus Award-winning se

Or visit WWW.VINZANDRI.COM to join 'Vincent's "Fo newsletter today.

PRAISE FOR VINCENT ZANDRI

"Sensational . . . masterful . . . brilliant."
—New York Post

"(A) chilling tale of obsessive love from Thriller Award–winner Zandri (Moonlight Weeps) . . . Riveting."
—Publishers Weekly

". . . Oh, what a story it is . . . Riveting . . . A terrific old school thriller."
—Booklist "Starred Review"

"Zandri does a fantastic job with this story. Not only does he scare the reader, but the horror Show he presents also scares the man who is the definition of the word "tough."
—Suspense Magazine

"I very highly recommend this book . . . It's a great crime drama that is full of action and intense suspense, along with some great twists . . . Vincent Zandri has become a huge name and just keeps pouring out one best seller after another."
—Life in Review

"(The Innocent) is a thriller that has depth and substance, wickedness and compassion."
—The Times-Union (Albany)

"The action never wanes."
—Fort Lauderdale Sun-Sentinel

"Gritty, fast-paced, lyrical and haunting."
—Harlan Coben, New York Times bestselling author of *Six Years*

"Tough, stylish, heartbreaking."
—Don Winslow, New York Times bestselling author of *Savages* and *Cartel.*

"A tightly crafted, smart, disturbing, elegantly crafted complex thriller . . . I dare you to start it and not keep reading."
—MJ Rose, New York Times bestselling author of *Halo Effect* and *Closure*

"A classic slice of raw pulp noir…"
—William Landay, New York Times bestselling author of *Defending Jacob*

"Zandri (is) a veteran wordsmith who executes quality and quantity at superlative levels."
—Book Reporter

American Crime Story

A Thriller Series: Book IV

Vincent Zandri

“People deserve a second chance, just like businesses.”

--Marty Byrde, Ozark

Book IV

1

Seconds Later

Joanne and Sean come running to the door. She screams and sprints down the steps and across the lawn, collapsing onto her son.

From down on my knees, I shout, "Sean, call nine-one-one! Do it now!"

But the son of a bitch hesitates.

"You sure that's a good idea, buddy?" he says. "I mean, that's got all the ear markings of a hit by Don Juan Perez. What the *hell* did you do to *piss* him off?"

I pat my back pocket, find my phone. My hands are trembling and there's blood on them. But I manage to dial 911. The dispatcher asks me to state the nature of my emergency. I tell her my son's been shot, and that he badly needs an ambulance right now.

"Is he breathing?" she asks.

I place my ear over his mouth.

"Yes," I say.

"Okay," she says. "Do not try to move him. What's your address?"

I tell her.

"Assistance is on the way, sir," she says.

The connection is cut. I stare down at my son. His eyes are rolling around in their sockets. He's trying to speak to me.

"Am I shot?" he mumbles, like his mouth has blood in it.

"Yes, son," I say, tears welling up in my eyes.

You've been shot and it is all your mom's and my fault...

"How…many…times," he asks, his words barely audible above Joanne's weeping.

"It looks like twice, Junior," I say.

"Direct…pressure," he says. "Apply…direct…pressure."

He barely gets the last word out before his eyes roll back in his head and he passes out.

Placing my hands on both entry wounds, I shout, "Don't you die on me, son! Stay with us!"

He's been shot in the left chest and lower pelvis area. I have both my hands pressed over both wounds, the blood seeping out from the narrow openings between my fingers. It dawns on me then that we can't be here when the EMTs and the police arrive. If we're here, they will arrest us, and we will be no good to Junior if we're in jail. But that's not the only reason we need to flee. If we're in jail, I have no doubt in my mind that Don Juan Perez will find a way to kill us all. After all, there are plenty of gangsters in jail and in New York State prisons. They will find us and kill us. It will be Perez's ultimate revenge.

Coming out of the distance now, sirens.

"Joanne!" I bark. "Listen to me. You've got to go back in the house. Retrieve the money from the closet and your gun. Do you hear me?"

She's not acknowledging me. She's just down on her knees, crying her eyes out.

"Joanne!" I scream. "You've got to listen to me."

She cries some more. That's when I do something I have never done in my life, nor ever thought of doing. I slap her across the face. She does something that takes me by surprise. She immediately stops crying. Raising her hand, she gently touches the spot on her face where I slapped her. In the exterior lamp light, I can see that the tips of her fingers are covered in our son's blood and some of it smears on her cheek.

Over her shoulder I see Sean just standing there in shock. He's gone from totally buzzed to stone cold sober. For once he has nothing to say. He's just standing there like a statue.

"You hit me," she says.

"I'm trying to get you to focus," I say. "You hear those sirens? That's not only an ambulance. That's the cops too. We will be arrested and charged with murder. So then, while I'm applying pressure to Junior's wounds, you and Sean go back to the house. Collect your gun, the money in the bedroom, and the phone chargers. Go now. Are we understanding one another, Joanne?"

Her fingers still touching her face, still smearing blood.

"Yes," is all she says.

Standing, she about-faces and heads for the front door. Sean follows on her bootheels. Meanwhile, I focus back on my son.

"Hang in there, kid," I plead. "Help is on the way."

"Dad," he says, his voice even weaker than before. "Who…shot…me?"

"Some bad people," I say. "Don't worry. You're gonna make it. I'm gonna get the people who did this to you."

"Don't get…yourself…killed," he says.

I'll be damned if he isn't trying to smile.

"That's my boy," I say, leaning into him, and kissing his forehead.

Joanne and Sean reappear at the front door. He's carrying the shoe boxes, and she's got her leather bag. I wave them towards me. Coming from out of the very near distance now, more sirens. Louder, more blaring sirens.

"Listen, Junior," I say, "the EMTs are here. Your mother and I have to leave. I'll explain it all later when you're better. But for now, we have to go. You will be in good care. You're going to your own emergency room."

That's when I feel my eyes well up for the second time. If I allowed myself, I could burst into tears on the spot. But the last thing I want my son to see is a weak father. Maybe I was a boring father when I was raising him. A stable father. And maybe I've changed a lot since those days. But I can also show him that I'm a stronger man than I used to be. Right now, he needs a strong, confident dad, or he won't make it.

"I love you," I say. "Never forget that."

Releasing my hands from his wounds, I dig in my back pocket for my handkerchief. I wipe as much of the blood as I can from my hands while going to Brad Junior's truck. Opening the passenger side door, I grab the plastic money bag. If I leave it here, the police will surely confiscate it for evidence once they make my entire property a crime scene. Coming back around the truck I gaze at my new Jeep and see that the back tires have been shot out. Both are flat. It's useless.

"Sean?" I bark. "Your Volkswagen! Now!"

He fumbles in his pockets for his keys.

"I hope I have gas," he says.

I snatch the keys out of his hands.

"You get in the back," I insist, heading for the car at the bottom of the driveway. "Joanne, you ride shotgun."

She turns once more, eyes her son lying on the lawn, bathed in a dark red pool of his own blood.

"I love you, Bradley!" she shouts, her face streaming with tears. "Please stay alive!"

For a quick second, I swear my son is trying to raise his right hand, as if to reassure his mother he's all right. He is far stronger than I ever gave him credit. I open the driver's side door of Sean's ride, toss the money bag to the passenger side floor. Slipping behind the wheel of the Volkswagen hatchback, I shove the key in the starter, and turn the engine over. I must believe my boy is going to live. If I don't believe that, I will die a slow death. Joanne will die an even slower death.

The sirens are getting so close I'm convinced we're not going to make it out of there on time.

"Get in!" I demand. "Hurry up!"

Sean opens the passenger side door, shoves himself and the shoeboxes of cash in the back seat. Joanne, her eyes never leaving her son, slowly sets herself down in the shotgun seat. She closes the door. She's openly weeping, her sobs breaking my heart. Shoving the floor-mounted joystick in reverse, I pound my foot on the gas and back out of the drive without bothering to look in the rearview or side mirrors.

Hitting the brakes, I press the tranny in drive, and punch the gas once more, the tires spitting gravel. We're heading further into the neighborhood.

"Where the hell are you going, Brad buddy?" Sean begs. "The main road is in the opposite direction."

My son is dying on the front lawn of the home he grew up in, and he's back to calling me *Brad buddy*.

"We go towards the main road, we'll run into a caravan of cops," I say.

"But there's no way out," Joanne says, wiping her eyes with the back of her hands. "It's a cul-de-sac."

"When there's a will," I say, and leave it at that.

I speed down the dark neighborhood road, until I spot Sean's split-level ranch. Tapping the brakes, I pull into his driveway.

"You're dropping me off, buddy, at a time like this?" he asks.

"No, Sean, pal," I say. "You're in for the long haul. You're not getting off that easy."

Pulling onto the lawn, I drive around the house, across the back lawn to a patch of woods that separates Sean's property from the backyard of a house located in the adjoining neighborhood. The headlamps lighting up the brush and the trees, I plow through the thick stuff like I'm driving a Sherman tank. Sideswiping a tree, I can feel the driver's side door panel cave in.

"Holy crap, Bradley," Sean spits, sitting up and sticking his head through the opening between the seats. "I was gonna trade this in for a Mercedes next week."

I have to admit, I can't help but feel a little glee, smashing Sean's ride up a little. Serves him right. Balling my wife in the basement. What was he thinking? That I would never find out about their affair?

"That is, you live to see next week, Sean pal," I say, the car bumping and pounding its way through the woods, the engine revving, the wheels spinning and slipping on the wet, muddy earth. "We are officially on the run from both the law and Don Juan Perez."

"But he's our partner in the Bubble Gum op," he says. "Surely all this is one big misunderstanding."

Joanne does something then that takes me by complete surprise.

"Listen, you drunk son of a bitch!" she barks over her shoulder. "My son is dying right now and it's all your fucking fault!"

I break through the woods, then plow through somebody's wood privacy fence. Speeding across the back lawn passed an in-ground pool, I crash through another section of fencing. Motoring across the side and front lawn, I end up on another neighborhood street called, Princess Lane. This street accesses the main north/south New York Route 9 via a connecting church parking lot. Gunning the Volkswagen, I turn onto the church lot which is empty at this time of day. I race across the lot, find the outlet to the road, and hook a left onto it.

We're free, for now.

"That's not fair, Joanne," Sean says, sitting back. "I had nothing to do with Bradley Junior getting shot."

"You got us into this," she says.

"You *asked* me to fucking get you into this," he spits.

He has a point. Joanne did ask him to get us into this.

"He's right, Jo," I say. "Nobody put a gun to our heads when we decided to enter the drug trade. We did it by our own accord, and now we're suffering the consequences."

She starts weeping again.

"I hope they're taking good care of our son," she says, through the tears. "If we lose him, I don't know how I can go on."

I place my hand on her leg, give it a squeeze.

"He's going to be fine," I say. "He's young and strong. By the looks of it, he wasn't hit in a vital spot."

Of course, I have no idea if this is true or not, but it seems like the right thing to say. It's also something I *want* to believe.

"How can you be sure?" she says, reaching into her purse and pulling out a fresh Kleenex. "You're just a mailman."

Oh, now that hurts…

She wipes her eyes and blows her nose. Removing my hand, I slap my now flat, hard belly.

"Because I feel it in my gut," I say. "He's not only going to live, he's going to have a full recovery. Trust me. Right now, he's probably telling the surgeons exactly what to do and how to do it."

We drive along Route 9 until we pass by the city, and the scenery becomes more rural and darker.

"Where are we going, Brad buddy?" Sean says after a time.

"Somewhere safe," I say. "We'll find a small motel in the Catskills away from it all and regroup. We'll make a plan."

"For what exactly?" Sean says.

"For killing Don Juan Perez," I say. "Before he kills us first."

"Bite the head off the snake," Joanne says. "The rest of the body dies."

"That would be the plan," I say.

"You both are crazy, you know that?" Sean says. "Don Juan Perez has access to a fucking army."

"We do too," I say. "He just doesn't know it yet. *You* don't know it yet."

A heavy silence fills the beat-up Volkswagen while we speed down a narrow road flanked by trees and the occasional farmhouse.

"I could really use a beer right now," Sean says after a time.

I glance at him in the rearview, at his puffy, sore black eye, and at his swollen face.

"Me too, buddy," I say. "Me too."

2

The darkness seems even darker and impenetrable by the time I enter the sleepy town of Catskill. When I spot a hardware store that's still open, I pull into the lot, and park just outside the front door.

"What are you doing?" Joanne asks. "Why aren't we calling the hospital and checking on Junior?"

"Because it's too risky," I say. "We're wanted fugitives. They're gonna wanna know who's calling and they're going to see our caller ID."

"Yeah, buddy," Sean says from the back seat. "What the hell are you doing? Maybe it's not a great idea to show your face in a store that's got CCTV."

"I'll be okay," I say. "I'll leave the engine running. And do not call the hospital."

My debit card is pretty spent after buying the new Jeep. But I have a little cash in my pocket, so there's no reason to retrieve any cash from the money bag or from the shoeboxes. Besides, what I'm buying isn't expensive. Opening the door, I get out and head into the store. An older man is standing behind the counter. He smiles at me as the bells connected to the door jingle all the way.

I take a quick look around the store. It's more a general store than a hardware store. It's got all sorts of tools and gadgets, but he also sells hunting boots, knives, rifles, and shotguns. Even AR15s. A small section is devoted to muzzle loaders. There's a big drawing of a bear over the muzzle loaders. It reads, "Bear Season is Coming Soon!" I'm standing in the heart of the Catskills. It's the mountain country where Bears are prevalent.

"Excuse me," I say, "where do you keep the duct tape?"

"Aisle three," the old man says. "You're lucky you caught me in time. I was just about to lock up for the night."

I make a quick check for CCTV cameras. Much as I hate to admit it, Sean's right. The last thing we need right now is for me to be videotaped. I don't see any. It doesn't mean they're not there, but I get the feeling the old man hasn't quite gotten around to installing a modern-day security system.

"I'll be quick," I say.

I head to aisle three, grab a roll of the thick gray tape and bring it back with me to the counter.

"Four fifty," he says.

I pull out a five. There's a TV sitting on a small table behind the counter, but it's not tuned into the news, thank God. I'm sure pictures of Joanne's and my face are all over the place by now. Maybe even across the entire U.S. Still, he's giving me this look with his bloodshot, brown eyes like he somehow recognizes me.

"Need a bag, Mister?" he asks.

"That would be great."

Maybe it's me, but he's moving very slow. He licks the tips of his fingers, then grabs a plastic bag off a stack set under the counter. He places the roll of duct tape inside the bag. He then picks up the five-dollar bill, opens the register, makes change, and hands it to me. There's a Feed the Children plastic bucket set on the counter, and I tell him to put the change in there.

"That's very generous, Mister," he says.

I grab the bag, turn, and head for the door.

"Say, Mister," he says.

Here it comes…

"Yeah," I say, looking not directly at him, but over my shoulder.

"I know you from somewhere?"

"Lots of people say I look like George Clooney in his younger days," I lie.

He chuckles.

"That must be it," he says.

I leave.

Getting back into the car, I can tell Joanne and Sean have been talking about their, let's call it relationship. I know this because she's crying again, and they immediately stop what they were saying when I open the door and slip back behind the wheel. To say the silence is as thick as it is awkward is putting it, well, mildly.

I set the bag of tape onto my wife's lap.

"What's this?" she says.

"Something I'm gonna need later," I say.

With that, I back up and continue south in search of a safe house.

3

Four or five miles down the road, I find a motel-no-tell, that fits the bill. It's got a big sign out front that says, The Rivera Motel, lit up in bright red neon. I pull up in front of the office and put the car in park, let the engine idle. Reaching down past Joanne's legs, I grab one of the stacks of cash, peel off three hundred bucks, then return the remainder of the stack not to the plastic bag, but my wife's leather bag.

"Be right back," I say.

Heading into the dimly lit office, I look for a human being behind the counter. But no one's there. That is, until a woman appears from behind a curtain that covers a door opening behind the counter. She's an older woman. Older than me, maybe by twenty years. She's very small, almost frail. Her hair is silver, and plastic yellow curlers seem to be holding it together. A pair of reading glasses are strapped to her neck with a thin silver chain. She's wearing a white housedress with little yellow and red flowers printed on it. Something my grandmother would have worn around her house just before bedtime.

"Help you?" she says, with a forced smile.

“I’d like a room with two beds,” I say.

She looks at me for a moment, and puts her reading glasses on. She then comes around the counter. That’s when I notice she’s wearing slippers. She walks over to the window wall, looks out at the still idling Volkswagen.

Coming back around the counter, she says, “That your car out there?”

“Yes, mam,” I say.

“You want one room for the three of you?” she asks. Leaning into me a little. “I can smell booze on your breath. You all planning on getting it on or something?” She raises her hand, extends her index finger, points it at me. “Listen, I don’t want no funny business. This is a family establishment, even if most of our clientele is truckers and sale’s people passing through.”

I smile. “Nothing like that. That man in the back seat of the car is my wife’s brother.”

“You say so,” she says with a smirk. She goes back around the counter, reaches under it, produces a clipboard with a questionnaire clipped to it. “Fill this out please.”

It’s the usual first and last name thing. Address. Type and model of automobile.

“A room on the very end would be preferable,” I say. “I’m a light sleeper.”

A wooden box that’s got about two dozen small wood boxes built into it, hangs on the wall beside the curtain.

“I think I can oblige,” she says.

She goes to the box, pulls out a key, sets it on the counter. That’s the room located all the way down opposite the office. Room 16. How many nights will you be staying?”

"One or two," I say. But I have no idea.

"How can you not know how many nights?" she asks suspiciously. "Say you're not in any kind of trouble, are you, Mister?"

She's giving me that look like the hardware salesman gave me a little while ago. A suspicious, *Where have I seen you before?* look.

"Not at all," I say. "We're just taking a road trip is all. No set schedule. Enjoying the early fall foliage. Enjoying ourselves."

Her eyes burn into mine for a long beat.

"I feel like I know you," she says.

Ok, so she said it. Exactly what I knew she would say if she decided to put her thoughts into words.

"Not sure how," I say. "I'm just a mailman. Nobody famous."

"Well," she says, shifting her eyes from me to her computer screen, "if you were famous, you wouldn't be staying in this dump." She hits a couple of keys on the keyboard, squints at the flatscreen. "It's seventy-five per night. How would you like to pay?"

I pull out one of the Benjamins.

"Cash okay?"

"I'd prefer it."

She takes the bill in hand, then goes under the counter again, comes back out with a strong box. Opening it, she makes twenty-five dollars change, and hands it to me.

“I like to use cash too,” I say. “Feels more honest.”

“Cash and honesty,” she says, returning the strong box to its place under the counter. “You must be like a saint or something. Maybe that’s how I know you.” Then, handing me the key. “If you want a decent place to eat, there’s VinceAnna’s down the road if you haven’t had your dinner yet. They serve till eleven, so you still got time. They do a real nice roast chicken. They have a good bar too. There’s a diner further on down the road for breakfast.”

“Thanks,” I say. “We ate a while ago. Think we’re just gonna hit the hay.”

She looks past me at the car again, lit up in the glow from the red neon sign.

“Well then, have a good night and enjoy your stay at the Riviera Motel.”

Key in hand, I head back out to the car. Nobody is saying a word. Sean looks like he’s going through alcohol withdrawal, and Joanne’s face is wet with tears.

“I need to know how Bradley is doing,” she says.

“We’re gonna find out right now on the news,” I say. “Let’s just get inside the room.”

I drive away from the office, pull up outside room number 16. We all get out and stand before the door.

“Jesus, I need a beer,” Sean says while cradling the shoeboxes full of cash.

Joanne and I ignore him. Slipping the key into the lock, I open the door and step inside. Joanne follows, her leather bag in hand. Then comes Sean. As soon as he sets the shoeboxes on the bed and closes the door behind him, I grab hold of his arm, wallop him in the stomach with a swift uppercut he never sees coming.

"That's for fucking my wife," I say, the adrenaline racing through my veins.

He's doubled over.

"Jeeze, Brad buddy," he spits, his voice painful, the air knocked out of him. "Why'd you have to go and do a thing like that?"

I follow with an upper cut to his chin. He drops onto the floor, out cold.

"And that's for selling us out to Don Juan," I say.

"Bradley!" Joanne scolds.

Her face is pale, eyes wide. She's in shock. But not because Bradley Junior has been shot. It's because she knows that I know, that she's been sleeping with Sean.

"How long you been sleeping with him, Jo?" I ask.

But she doesn't answer. She just looks at me, her mouth agape, her lower jaw hanging somewhere down around her sternum.

"I…I…," she stammers.

"You know what?" I say. "Don't even answer that. I'm not sure I wanna know. But what I would like to know is if you're aware that Sean has been selling us out to Don Juan?"

"I have no idea about something like that, Bradley," she says, her expression now taking on an angrier tone, like she's insulted I'd even suggest it. "How do you know he's been selling us out?"

I slap my mid-section again.

"My gut tells me it's so. That shiner he's got? That's not because of running into a door jamb. It's because Don Juan's people must have roughed him up for information. Perez sent me some texts earlier tonight that prove he's finally figured out where he last saw me, which was where you killed his little brothers. I was delivering mail to Mark and his wife at Little's Lake. Or pretending to anyway. And when he saw the FBI wanted poster with my face on it and yours, he must have put it all together. He pulled Sean in and made him talk, just to be sure we were the ones who not only killed his brothers but also Mark and Melanie." I gently kick Sean with my boot tip. "Sean killed them anyway. But we're gonna take the rap for being coconspirators. You know that don't you?"

Joanne is back to crying again. I look around the room. There're two beds, a small table and two chairs, and a long dresser of drawers. Mounted on the wall over the dresser, is a flatscreen TV. A remote control is sitting on the dresser. I grab it and press the green ON button.

"I need you to go back in the car and grab the bag from the hardware store, Jo," I say.

She wipes her eyes while I try and find the channel for Spectrum News.

"What are you doing?" she asks, stepping past me.

"Trying to find out if anything about our son is being reported."

She opens the door, steps out into the night. When she comes back in, she's got the plastic bag in hand. She closes the door, and sets the bag on the table.

"Apply the deadbolt," I insist. "You never know who might have followed us here."

I also ask her to plug the phone chargers into the outlets located on the wall between the beds, and to plug the phones in. Meantime, I finally find the Spectrum 24-hour news. But what they're reporting on has nothing to do with our son.

Going to the bag, Joanne opens it, pulls out the roll of duct tape.

"What are you gonna do with this, Brad?" she asks.

"Help me get him up and into one of those chairs by the window."

I fully expect her to complain, but she doesn't. She just quietly assists me with lifting Sean's deadweight and shoving him in the chair closest to the wall.

"Now," I say, tearing the clear plastic off the roll of tape, "wrap him up in duct tape so he can't get away."

"You really think he'll try and get away?" she asks, peeling back some tape, sticking it to his left arm, and then proceeding to wrap it all the way around his chest and then the back of the chair.

"When he wakes up and hears what I'm about to tell him," I say, "he's most definitely going to want to run."

She's wrapped the tape around him maybe six or seven times, before she tears her end off.

"Now get his ankles," I say.

She drops to her knees, wraps some of the tape around his ankles. Standing, she drops the tape onto the table.

“He’s going nowhere.”

That’s when he starts to come around. He’s bobbing his head up and down, his eyes partially open.

“Beer,” he mumbles. “I want a beer, buddy.”

“So, what are you going to tell him, Brad?” she says.

“The same thing I’m about to tell you.”

“And that is?”

“Tonight, this thing ends. I’m calling Detective Danish and confessing everything. I don’t give a shit what happens to us. I only care if Brad Junior makes it out of this alive.”

“I thought you wanted to kill Perez,” she says. “Bite the head off the snake.”

“I’ve changed my mind,” I say. “Don’t you think enough people are dead?”

“So long as one of them isn’t my son,” she says.

“I couldn’t agree more,” I say.

4

The Spectrum News switches over to a commercial.

"There's got to be something on Brad Junior by now," I say.

"Why don't we just call the hospital for God's sakes."

"I don't want to take that chance, Jo. Not yet. They'll have our number and voices on record."

"We can use the motel phone," she pushes.

"Just hang on," I insist.

Joanne is standing between the duct tape-bound Sean and the small round plastic table. Her arms are crossed tightly over her chest. Meanwhile, Sean is back to more or less passed out.

"I'm sorry, Bradley," she says.

"What for?" I say. "For deciding to become a drug runner?"

"No," she says. "For what happened with Sean. I didn't want you to know."

"So how long has it been going on?" I ask again.

"Not long," she says. "A few weeks. I guess I just got caught up in the excitement of everything and then, it just sort of happened. I feel like what we've been doing…the life we've been living, the money we've been making…it's like I've been living inside a Netflix show." She tears up again. "And then our son goes and gets shot."

"How's that for a dose of reality?" I say.

I'm holding the remote in my hand. I'm squeezing it so tight, I feel like I could crush it. The news comes back on. The same young woman who's been reporting on the local murders of the Perez brothers and the Camps is holding a microphone to her face just outside our Hope Street house.

"Here it is," I say. "Pray to God he's all right."

"As we've been reporting all evening, earlier tonight, a local physician was cut down by a drive-by shooting," she says into her mic. "Doctor in Residence, Bradley Jones, Junior, twenty-eight of Albany, was shot twice. Once in the chest and once in the upper pelvic region. While Jones's condition is considered critical now, doctors tell us he is stable and his injuries non-life threatening since no vital organs were damaged. He did however, lose considerable blood and several bones were broken, along with a collapsed left lung."

"Thank God," my wife says through her tears.

I, on the other hand, say nothing, because I'm afraid I'll burst out crying if I do. That's how happy I am. My son is going to live and that means all the world to me. I just hope he'll find it in his heart to forgive us for having to run out on him, the way we did. But then, what choice did we have? There was never any choice.

"The precise reason for the shooting," the reporter goes on, "remains unclear. However, what is becoming more and more clear, is this: the residents of this humble home on Hope Street in a sleepy hamlet of North Albany, Bradley Jones and Joanne Jones, both fifty-eight years of age, are now the major suspects not only in the killings of the Perez Brothers some months back, but also in the murders of Mark and Melanie Camp. That is, according to testimony by Albany Homicide Detective, David Danish. They are also suspected of having become mixed up in a rival drug war with suspected cartel member, Juan Perez, older brother of the slain gang members, Hector and Julio Perez. Up until recently, Bradley Jones was a near thirty-five-year veteran of the postal service with a stellar record of conduct. Mrs. Jones was a housewife who occasionally volunteered at the Albany Public Library. How the two seemingly mild mannered, middle-aged couple got caught up in a drug war, is for anyone to speculate, states Danish. But it is indeed strange, and by all accounts, tragic due the severe wounding of their son, and the killings of four Albany residents."

The reporter signs off. It's at that precise time, my phone vibrates in my pocket.

"Well, thank God my name didn't come up, Brad buddy," a suddenly awake Sean says from the chair he's bound to. He's been watching the report the entire time. "Thank God for small miracles, huh? Now, you gonna untie me?"

Joanne does something that shocks me then. She steps around the front of the chair and, facing Sean, she hauls off and slaps him across the face. She hits him so hard I can almost feel it.

"You bastard," she says. "You haven't even mentioned our son. He wouldn't be shot if it wasn't for you."

Sean's got a bright red cheek to go with that shiner of an eye. But he looks more hurt by Joanne's anger than the slap.

"Why'd you have to go and hit me, Jo honey?" he spits.

Jo honey...He's got to be kidding... I'm standing right here...

"You've been talking to Juan Perez," she says. "You told him we killed his brothers. His men forced it out of you. You either confessed or they were gonna kill you. Chop you up or something."

"I did no such thing," Sean insists, but I can tell by the way his eyes are rolling around in their sockets that he's a lying sack of shit.

He knows we know he's lying. I glance at my phone. It's another couple messages from Perez. My pulse picks up, mouth goes dry.

"Brad buddy," Sean says. "You don't believe what Joanne is saying, do ya? I would never rat you guys out to save my own skin. Come on, how long have we been friends?"

Glancing up from my phone.

"Joanne," I say, "gag our old friend before he makes me shoot him."

She picks up the roll of tape, tears off a long piece and wraps it around Sean's entire head, including his big mouth. His eyes go wide, and he starts yelling into the tape, but his voice is entirely muted. That's a good thing. I shift my eyes back to my phone. What I see is fire. Our new funeral home is going up in flames.

Turning the phone around so that Joanne and our business partner can see what's happening to our combo funeral parlor/Bubble gum cooking facility. "Behold what's left of our business, folks."

Joanne's face goes so tight I'm afraid it might split down the center. She's so angry right now, I'm surprised she's not using Sean's head for a speed bag. Speaking of Sean, his eyes also go wide. He starts shouting into his gag. I have no idea what he's saying, but I can tell it's something about his having nothing to do with the fire.

Another photo comes through. It's an image of our Russian friend, Lurch, along with Smirking Jack and Thin Jay. They are wearing Hazmat suits and holding their gas masks in their hands. Randy is smirking as usual, while the others stare at the camera with deadpan expressions. There's someone else in the photo standing beside them. Someone I've never seen before, but whom I suspect is Sean's old Russian boss, Carcov. Why do I believe this? Because I'll be damned if he doesn't fit the cliched image of the TV Russian gangster. He's tall, and heavy in the middle. His hair is white and slicked back on his round head with gel. The navy-blue Nike track suit he's wearing is too small, and his gut protrudes from it. His eyes are covered in RayBan aviator sunglasses, and he's got a couple thick silver chains hanging off his neck.

Turning the phone around so Sean can see the picture.

"Carcov," I say. "Is that him?"

He tries to say something through the gag.

"Just nod your head," I insist. "Yes or no." Eyes wide, he nods his head. Turning the phone screen back around. "So, the head Russian is now personally teaming up with the head

Mexican. That way they cut us out entirely. Makes sense, I guess." My eyes back on Sean. "Let me guess, old buddy, you helped facilitate the deal."

His eyes even wider, he shouts something into the tape. Something like, "I can explain," or "What choice did I have, they had a gun to my head," or "They were gonna torture me."

Anyway, doesn't matter now, does it?

Behind Carcov and the other three now former Fitzgerald Funeral Home workers is a sophisticated menagerie of stainless-steel drug cooking apparatus that makes the setup we had in the basement of the funeral parlor look like a junior high toy chemistry set.

I say, "I can bet Don Juan and Carcov are paying our former employees a hell of a lot more than we were paying them. Looks like he was going to pay Sean too. Isn't that right, old buddy?"

"Don Juan can afford it," Joanne says. "We don't have Don Juan's hundreds of millions. Not yet."

Another text comes from Don Juan. This one is words only.

"You can't hide, gringo. When the time is right, I will find you and you will know what it's like to be in pain for a long time before you die."

My body is trembling. My eyes are not focused on the digital smartphone screen, but instead, glued to it. I'm reading his words over and over again, but they never change. What I'm living right now is not a nightmare. It is much worse because it is reality. It means I'm not going to wake up.

"What is it?" Joanne says. "What else is he saying, Bradley?"

Finally, I pull my eyes away from the phone and glance at her.

"I think he knows where we are," I say, my mouth so parched, the words hardly coming out.

Sean's eyes are wide open. Even the black and blue one. His face is so red, it's possible he's going to burst a blood vessel in his brain. Couldn't happen to a nicer guy.

"What do you mean he knows where we are?" Joanne goes on.

"He has people all over the place," I say. "If you want to call them people. Human beings are people. The animals we're going to be dealing with are not human."

But that's when something hits me over the head. Shoving my phone in my back pocket, I go to the door, open it, and head outside. Pulling my smartphone out, I depress the flashlight icon. Going around the back of Sean's Volkswagen hatchback, I drop to one knee and spray the bright LED light under the back bumper. It takes maybe a second and a half for me to find it. A LoJack tracking device. Yanking it off the bumper, I straighten up, then toss the device to the gravel covered ground and stomp on it with my boot heel. Killing the flashlight app, I shove the phone back in my pocket.

"This is all my fault," I whisper to myself. "I should have never trusted Sean. Never trusted this entire scheme. Maybe I should not have trusted my wife either."

Heading back inside, I see Joanne draw the curtains closed on the window over the round table.

"You mean they could be looking in at us right now, Bradley?"

I tell her about the LoJack.

“They could be surrounding us right now,” I say. “Or maybe they still haven’t yet caught up to us. But there is one thing I do know.”

She folds her arms tightly around her chest again.

“What is it, Bradley?” she asks.

My eyes back on my phone.

“I’m calling Danish,” I say. “This ends now. We need police protection, and we need it now, Joanne.”

I don’t know Danish’s private line, but all I have to do is look up the APD, Central Avenue Precinct, and the dispatcher will connect me with at least his mailbox. If my gut instinct is right on, Danish is the type to check his messages at all hours of the night. I press the Alexa icon.

“Alexa,” I say into the phone, “find me the phone number for the Albany Police Department, Central Avenue Precinct.”

Alexa not only spits the number out, but it appears on the screen. All I’m required to do is tap on it with the pad of my index finger. Heart beating in my throat, I tap the number, then place the phone to my ear.

That’s when I hear, “Bradley, please put the phone down, honey.”

I shoot my wife a quick glance. What I see doesn’t shock me, so much as breaks my heart in two even worse than watching her T-boning Sean. My wife is holding her gun on me.

“I mean it, Bradley, hang up the phone,” she demands.

I can hear the ringing coming over the connection.

"Why are you doing this, Jo?" I ask. "It's our only chance to get out of this alive."

She raises the gun, aims it directly at my face. If she shoots me at pointblank range, she'll evaporate my head like JFK in Dallas. Sucking in a deep breath, I press the end call icon, store the phone in my back pocket.

"We get the cops involved, we'll go away for life. *I'll* go away for life. But we both know life is a joke, since Perez will have us both killed inside prison. He'll stop at nothing to see us dead. And if he doesn't succeed, maybe Carcov will. Isn't that why we ran from the police in the first place? Isn't that why we left our son all alone, bleeding out on the front lawn?"

She's right, of course. Either way, Juan Perez will kill us. Doesn't matter if we call Detective Danish and confess. Perez has his sights set on us and that's that.

"So, what you're saying is we really do need to kill Perez before he gets to us," I say, like a question.

"Something like that," she says.

"Back to biting the head off the snake."

"It was your original plan," she says. "Your gut plan. We should stick with it instead of going back and forth on the issue. The world isn't big enough for us to hide in."

I nod, but then I'm not sure it matters if I agree with my wife or not.

"You gonna keep that thing pointed at me all night, Jo?"

She lowers the gun, shoves the barrel into her pant waist. For a second or two, we just stand there looking at one another inside that cramped motel room like we're seeing each other for the very first time. When a vehicle pulls up outside the window, the tires squealing against the pavement, we don't have time to take cover. The explosive hail of rapid-fire rounds shatters the picture window into a thousand little pieces.

5

My gut reaction is to lunge over Sean, grab hold of Joanne, drag her into the bathroom. But I end up tackling her, protecting her with my body. The hail of gunfire is ravaging the entire room. The TV and the dresser below it shatter. The shoeboxes full of cash are blown to bits, the cash shredding and blowing around the room like confetti. Bits of foam, fabric, and springs from the now destroyed mattress are spraying in all directions like shrapnel from a detonated bomb. The lamps get hit and the room goes dark. It's so loud and violent, it's like a war zone.

Sean is panicking, doing his best to bust out of the chair. I extend my leg and attempt to knock the chair over so that he has some protection. But just as I'm about to push him over with my boot heel, a round nails him squarely in the back of his head. The bullet takes most of his face off when it exits. Just like that, my business partner, former football Sunday afternoon drinking buddy, and my wife's illicit lover ceases to exist on planet earth.

As quickly as the shooting starts, it stops, the vehicle the bullets came from not peeling out for a quick getaway, but from the sounds of it, slowly moving forward, as though its driver and its occupants don't care about the police, but instead are more concerned with looking for any signs of life.

"Stay down, Jo," I insist.

On the bright side of things, the motel room is dark. It allows me to peek out the window. What I'm looking at is a big black Chevy Suburban with tinted windows. A bald, tattooed, young Latino man is driving. His window is rolled all the way down.

"Who are they?" Joanne says from down on her back.

"It's Perez all right," I say. "And here I thought they wanted to torture us first."

"Looks like Juan wanted to expedite our execution," she says. "Can't say I blame him." She hesitates a little. "Wait a minute," she adds, lifting her hand. "Is that blood on my fingers?"

Apparently, she has no idea about Sean.

"Sean," is all I say.

"Sweet Jesus, is he dead?"

"He took one in the back of the head, Jo," I say. "I'm sorry."

That's when she shifts and lifts herself off the floor. Meanwhile, the Suburban makes its way across the lot and turns onto the main road, heading north in the direction of Albany. I go to the wall mounted light switch by the door, push them all up. Two dim, ceiling mounted cans turn on near the bathroom. Joanne looks at what's left of Sean's head, his brains and facial skin staining the shot-up bed. Shoving herself past the corpse, she hops over all the shattered glass on her way to the bathroom and heaves her spaghetti dinner.

I go to Sean, feel around his backside for his pistol. When I find it, I shove the barrel into my front pant waist. I pat his pockets and find an extra magazine. I shove that into my jeans pocket. It begins to dawn on me that maybe Joanne was right. Going to the police is a bad idea. But this thing still ends today. Tonight. That means one thing. If we're going to bite the head off the snake, we need to go directly to the snake.

My wife emerges from out of the bathroom. She's drying her hands and face with a towel. She's also averting her eyes from what's left of Sean's head.

"Grab your bag and your phone," I say. "We're leaving before the police get here."

She tosses the towel back inside the bathroom.

"So soon?" she says, both her hands trembling.

At least she's still got a sense of humor.

"The police have got to be on their way," I say. "This is the country, so it's gonna be a minute. But that's all. Just a minute. So come on, we have to go."

Digging into my pocket for Sean's car keys, I go to the door, undo the dead bolt. The bullets made Swiss cheese out of the cheap wood door panel. Some of the red neon is spilling through the holes like laser beams. I open the door, step out to see the lot occupied by a scattering of motel residents and the owner herself, still dressed in her housecoat. She's carrying a baseball bat in her hand.

"You!" she screams while I press the button on the key fob that electronically unlocks the door. "I knew you was trouble the first time I set eyes on you."

"Get in the car, Jo," I say.

She opens the door, tosses her bag on the floor, and plants herself in the passenger seat. As I go around the Volkswagen, I can see that the hatchback glass has been hit by a stray bullet or two and shattered. I guess it's illegal to drive it in that condition, but we're up to our eyeballs in illegalities. And to think my ongoing relationship with Detective Danish started with a broken taillight on my minivan. It all seems like one hundred years ago. At least the tires look to be in good shape.

I open the driver's side door, jump in, and fire up the engine. Out the now open hatchback, I can make out the sound of sirens. I'm guessing out here in the sticks it will be the State Police who will answer the call. Throwing the tranny in reverse, I back out fast and pray no one is behind me. Then, shifting into drive, I peel out.

"Grab me a stack of cash," I say.

"How much?" Joanne asks.

"Just give me a stack."

I hit the brakes as I pull up beside the old woman. Joanne hands me the cash from the plastic bag stored in her leather bag. I peel off half the stack, and hand it to her in the red light of the bright neon sign.

"That's five thousand dollars," I say. "It should cover all the damages and then some."

She just looks at the cash in her hand like it's the most cash she's ever seen in her life.

"Just do me a favor," I say. "Don't tell the police what kind of car we're driving and which direction we went. We're the good guys, believe it or not."

She just nods. Of course, I don't know how good we really are. In the eyes of God, I'd say we're pretty bad. But compared to Don Juan Perez and his gang of cartel drug running gangbangers, we look positively angelic.

The sirens are getting a lot louder.

"We have to go, Bradley," Joanne says, anxiously.

I hit the gas. We race out of the Riviera Motel parking lot like a burning bat out of hell.

6

We're not three hundred feet away from the motel when I spot the rooftop flashers on not one, but two state trooper cruisers in the rearview. Or what I'm guessing are state troopers since we're all the way out in the sticks where no regular police force exists. At first, I feel like they're about to pursue us, and a wave of ice-cold water races up my spine. But when they pull into the motel lot, I know we're in the clear. At least for now.

"Now what?" Joanne asks.

For a time, I don't say a word. I just concentrate on the dark, winding country road ahead of me, the bright white light from the halogen headlamps cutting through it like flame through a black curtain.

Then, "Do you think God is on our side, Joanne?" I ask. "I mean, after everything we've done, the people we've killed, the money we stole, the drugs we sold, after our son taking two bullets…do you think God still likes us more than he does someone like Don Juan or Carcov?"

She turns to me. I shoot her a quick glance over my shoulder.

“Why would you ask a question like that?” she answers. “Of course, he likes us more. He loves us.”

“But we’ve done some pretty bad things, Jo.”

“I think of the bad things as things we had to do for the greater good.”

Shooting her another glance. “Like killing the Camps?”

“Okay,” she says, “maybe that wasn’t so great. But Sean did the actual killing, and as far as I know, it was only a suggestion. I wasn’t actually convinced he was going to go through with it.”

I’m not sure whether to believe her explanation or not. Or whether she believes it herself. Maybe it’s something she’s convinced herself of just for the sake of sanity. God knows how much she’s changed over the past few months, how much she has shed her old Joanne skin. It was the skin of an aging, timid, nearsighted middle-aged woman who drove like an old lady, looked after her mother, and who’s only ambition in life was to volunteer at the local library. Now she’s a killer, a drug runner, a money launderer, and a cheating wife.

Maybe she was all of these things all along, but only recently did everything come out. Kind of like a caterpillar that stays in its cocoon for far too long before sprouting its wings into a big, bright butterfly. But then, I’ve changed too. Maybe I haven’t cheated on Joanne, but I’m just as guilty as she is for a whole lot of crimes. One day, we’ll pay for our sins. But right now, more sins require committing.

We come to a red traffic light. Up ahead, is a small pocket of commercial buildings. There’s the hardware store where I bought the duct tape earlier. I’m also seeing a McDonalds, and a Stewarts gas station-slash-bread and butter shop. When the light turns green, I slowly proceed through the intersection. What I see at the gas station raises the hackles on the back of my neck.

It's a big black Suburban, and a stocky young gangster with shaved head covered in tattoos is presently filling his tank.

7

Heart jumps into my throat.

"Joanne," I say. "Look."

She peers out the passenger side window.

"Jesus, Mary, and Joseph," she says. "It's them."

I drive past the gas station, but then pull into the McDonald's parking lot directly next door. Here's what's going through my speeding brain: For certain, the gangster, along with the gangsters hiding behind all that tinted glass, are the same gangsters who just shot up our hotel room and killed Sean. But are they also the same ones who tried to kill my son? My gut, it's speaking to me again. It says, *"Yes, Bradley. The motherfuckers are one in the same."*

My beating heart fills not with blood, but rage. But here's what else fills my veins. An epiphany of sorts.

“Listen, Jo,” I say, “what if we do one more bad thing in the name of all that’s good and decent in this world?”

I listen to the idling engine while Joanne stares at the young gangster. He’s pumping the gas with one hand and looking at stuff on his iPhone with the other. He’s got a big smile on his face, like he’s having a fun night. Just then, a flash of lightning. It takes me and Joanne a little by surprise. It’s followed by some rain drops that pelt the windshield. Then comes the thunder. It’s an unexpected, Fall thunderstorm. A change of weather storm.

“What if we shoot back?” I say.

“We shoot back?” Joanne questions.

“Kill the drive-by shooters with a drive-by shooting of our own.”

Scooching up, I pull out Sean’s 9mm. I might be a post office nerd deep down inside, but I accompanied Sean more than once to the range. Rather, he’d drag me to the range, not kicking and screaming necessarily because I really like guns, but so that we’d have something else to do besides drink beer and watch football. The point being, I’ve shot this very pistol maybe a half dozen times before. I’ve also fired his AR15 and had a lot of fun doing it. It means I’m familiar with both weapons. But I wonder about my wife.

“Your gun,” I say. “You know how to use it?”

“Sean showed me,” she says, grabbing it out of her bag. “He’s been giving me shooting lessons for weeks, including firing his AR…AR…”

“AR Fifteen,” I interject.

“That’s it,” she says.

He showed you a lot of things, I want to say, but I rein myself in.

She pulls the slide back on her pistol just enough to show me she's got a round stored in the chamber. I guess she does know what she's doing. But it's yet one more thing about my wife that's so different from the woman she used to be. Not too long ago, she never in a million years would have considered owning a gun, much less having the know-how to keep a round stored in the chamber to get it off quick should a drug crazed bad guy be coming after her.

I give her a long, hard look.

"What?" she says.

"Who are you?" I say.

As if God timed it this way, lightning strikes again, and then comes the thunder. The rain is now pelting the windshield. I turn on the wipers. They make a rhythmic swishing sound as they clear the windshield of rainwater.

Joanne makes a sly grin.

"We've all changed, Bradley," she says. "You too have become a different man. But one thing hasn't changed. I still love you. I know I did a bad thing with Sean." She shakes her head, and I see the reflection of the gas station/convenience store exterior lights in the tears filling her eyes. "I seriously don't know what came over me when he and I…" Her voice trails off. "Well, you know."

"Yes," I say, somberly. "I know. I saw it with my own two eyes."

"Now Brad Junior is shot, and I feel responsible," she says. Placing her free hand on my thigh. "Will you ever forgive me, Bradley?"

In my head, I see the bullet penetrating Sean's head, his brains and facial tissue spattering all over the shot-up bed. He's out of our lives now. Gone forever, just like those shoe boxes filled with all that cash. So yeah, maybe it sucks that my wife was balling another man. But he's dead, and when this thing is finished, if we're not dead yet, she and my son will be all I'll have left in the world. They will be all I think about when they slam those steel prison doors shut on my cell at night.

I set my hand on hers, and squeeze it. In my mind, it's answer enough to her question.

Another lightning strike and more thunder. A blast of wind buffet's the car. Tattooed Gangster replaces the nozzle to the gas pump, and takes his printed receipt from the pump dispenser, shoves it into the pocket on his overly baggy jeans. He then opens the driver's side door on the Suburban, hops inside, slams the door closed. Firing the engine up, he pulls out of the pump station and crosses the lot to the main road.

"Let's do this," I say.

Joanne slips her hand off my thigh, and I back out of the parking space, put the transmission in drive and head for the road. The rain is steady now, and still coming down heavy. I put the wipers on the highest setting they will go and turn onto the road, heading south in the same direction as the Perez gangbangers.

This is the country, so I'm able to maintain a decent enough distance between them without losing sight of their taillights. More lightning strikes, more thunder, more rain. To be perfectly honest, I couldn't ask for better weather.

Joanne is nervously holding her short-barreled semi-automatic in her hand.

"What's the plan, Bradley?" she asks.

"I know it's not much of a plan," I say. "But just follow my lead. Eventually they're going to have to stop at a red light. When that happens, we pull up beside them, and let them have it."

"You sound like Jimmy Cagney in some old black and white gangster movie."

"Take a good look around you," I say. "We *are* in a black and white gangster movie."

We drive for another few miles. I'm doing about fifty. The road is winding and thick with second growth woods that flank it. The thunder and lightning have pretty much moved on, but the rain is still coming down hard. Up head, maybe a quarter mile in the distance, a traffic light. It's signaling green right now, but if I had to guess, by the time the Suburban pulls up to it, it will turn red.

I give the Volkswagen more gas. The car speeds up. It only takes a few seconds to come up on the Suburban's tail.

"Get ready," I say. "When they stop, I'm going to pull around them. We get out. I shoot the driver and you go for the passenger in the shotgun seat. We also take out the assholes in the back. Don't stop shooting until I tell you to. You got it?"

I shoot her a quick glance. Her eyes are wide open. If she had an Adam's apple it would be bobbing up and down in her neck. Her pulse must be pounding. I know mine is. A quick glance at my watch. It's a little past eleven. If this were even four months ago, I would be in bed on my back, my eyes struggling to stay open, but sleep overtaking them. My belly would be full from a dinner of Hamburger Helper or maybe meatloaf, and too much cheap beer. I would place my hand on it and feel the extra layer of fat.

Joanne would still be sitting up in bed, her readers covering her eyes while she watches another episode of some crime series on Netflix. Her favorite shows were about ordinary people thrust into extraordinary circumstances. Nice, God-fearing people, forced to take on a life of crime. It all seemed so far-fetched to me at the time, I never paid much attention to them. I just lived my day-to-day existence, delivering the mail and minding my own business, and at the same time, always carrying around the worry over a bank account that was constantly in the red. But that was then, and this is now.

The traffic light turns red. The driver of the Suburban hits the brakes. The white taillights are now accompanied by bright red brake lights. I too hit the brakes.

"This is it," I say. "Remember, don't stop shooting until I tell you too. And whatever we do, let's not shoot one another in the crossfire by mistake. Make sure you shoot into the vehicle but not at me. I'll do the same."

"Okay," she says. "Let's just get it over with already."

The Suburban comes to a full stop. That's when I turn the wheel sharply, and pull all the way around it, blocking it from going forward.

8

Throw open my door.

"Now, Joanne!" I bark.

She throws open her door. Our guns in hand, she goes around to passenger side of the Suburban and I take the driver's side. In a word, we light the vehicle up. I shoot both the driver's side window out and then the window in the back seat. I shoot the driver in the shoulder, and the gangster in the backseat in the face. He doesn't even have time to go for his gun. I see another bald headed, tattooed man fall onto his lap. Half his head is missing. Joanne is a hell of a shot it turns out.

I can see that she's shooting the gangster riding shotgun to bits.

"He's dead, Joanne!" I shout. "Hold your fire!"

The driver goes for his gun, but I shoot it out of his hand. His shoulder is spurting blood. Opening the door for him, I yank on his arm, and pull him out. He spills out onto the pavement.

He's in so much pain, his facial muscles are contorting. I step on his injured shoulder and the scream he produces echoes throughout the valley.

"Joanne," I say, "you didn't happen to remember the duct tape."

"In my bag," she says.

"Good, girl," I say. "Help me get him into the Volkswagen."

She takes hold of his other arm, and together, we drag the short, skinny gangster to the car. Opening the back door, we stuff him inside.

"The tape," I say.

She goes to the passenger side door, opens it, grabs the tape from her bag.

"Tear me off a long piece," I say.

She does it, hands it to me. I wrap it around his ankles.

"Another," I insist.

She hands me that one.

Grabbing both his wrists, I shove them around his lower back. He screams again from the pain.

"Tape his wrists, Joe," I say.

She scooches into the door opening and manages to wrap the tape tightly around his wrists. When it's done, we both back step out of the car and stand up straight. I look over both shoulders to make sure we're not being watched or followed. Thank God this is such a desolate place, or we'd have witnesses up our asses.

"Let's just go," I say.

I go around the car and slip back behind the wheel. Jo gets back into the passenger seat. After putting her seatbelt on, she reaches into her bag, comes back out with another full magazine. Thumbing the pistol's magazine release, she drops the empty mag into the bag, then slaps the full one in. She cocks back the slide, allows a bullet to enter the chamber. She thumbs the safety on while keeping the gun gripped in her shooting hand. My wife is taking no chances with this gangster…this *gangbanger*…even if he is tied up and bleeding all over Sean's ride, not that Sean gives a shit at this point.

The car is still idling, so all I have to do is throw the stick into drive and pull away. But something hits me then. Something I should avoid, but on the other hand, cannot resist.

"Hang on, Jo," I say, getting back out of the car, and walking to the shot-up Suburban. Pulling out my smartphone, I press the camera icon, snap a few pictures of the carnage. I then open the texts and send them on to Perez. My heart is pounding a mile a minute and I feel a wave of pure glee flow through my body. Maybe it's the reckless thing to do, but it feels so fucking good.

Just to add insult to grave injury, I type, "Nice try, asshole. You don't know who you're dealing with."

Heading back to the car, I get in, set the phone in the console cup holder. I put the transmission in drive and pull ahead. I don't drive fifty feet before I hear the phone vibrate and chime. I retrieve the phone while keeping my eyes on the country road. It's a text from Don Juan. I can't help but smile when I open it. But the picture he's sent wipes that smile off my face, just as quickly as it formed.

It's a photo of Joanne's mother. She's down on her knees, her body naked, her wrists duct taped to her ankles, a piece of the gray tape covering her mouth. Another photo arrives. It's my son. He's lying on a gurney, but he's obviously not inside a hospital room. He's inside what looks to be a concrete basement. His eyes are closed, like he's unconscious and he's hooked up to an IV. His face is pale and sickly looking under his black beard. Perez follows up with another text. This one only words.

"As you Americans like to say, gringo, right back atcha."

My stomach goes tight, and I feel a little nauseous. How the hell did he manage to steal two people right out from under the noses of both a major medical facility and a senior living facility? I guess if you employ the right people and spread around enough cash, you can do anything.

"What is it?" Joanne says. "You look like you just saw a ghost."

She doesn't know how close she's come to the truth. Do I tell her what's going on? That Don Juan has abducted her mother? Or do I let it go? Coming from the back seat, the sound of moaning. The gangster is coming around.

"Where are you taking me, gringo?" he whispers in a hoarse, painful voice. "When Don Juan finds out about this, he will kill you both. We are family. He will skin you both alive."

Joanne turns quick, aims her pistol barrel at him.

"Shut your mouth," she says. "You are in no position to make threats, young man."

He spits.

"Puta," he says, "I will fuck you and skin you myself."

"Tape his mouth," I say.

Joanne reaches into her bag, pulls out the tape. Instead of tearing a piece off, she unbuckles her seatbelt, turns herself around, reaches into the back with the tape and wraps it around his entire head and face six or seven times. Coming back around, she drops the tape in her bag.

"That will quiet him down for now," she says, a satisfied smile covering her face.

That's when I inhale a deep breath.

"Joanne," I say. "We gotta talk."

9

“How the hell did he even know I still have my mother?” Joanne asks, her voice tense and tight. “How did he take our son without the police knowing about it? Doesn’t the hospital have security? Why didn’t the police keep an armed guard in front of his room?”

She’s bordering on hysterical, and I can’t blame her.

“He knows everything about us. He’s Mexican cartel. They have the money and the connections to find out everything and anything they want. How do you think Don Juan has avoided prison for all these years when the police and the FBI know exactly what he is and what he does? Besides…”

“Besides what?” she asks, her tone filled with acid.

“Cops can be bought. Politicians can be bought. District Attorneys and judges can be bought.”

"First they shoot, Bradley," she says after a long beat. "And now they steal him. Then they take my mom. They…Perez and his men…he's going to kill them."

"This is war, Joanne," I say. "We have declared a war with Don Juan Perez. A fucking drug war." I find myself shaking my head in disbelief. "A few months ago, we were a simple family living in the suburbs. Today we're in a drug war. You can't make this shit up."

"So, how can we win this war and save my mother and our son?"

I turn off the country road and onto the ramp for the highway that will take us back to the city. The rain stops suddenly, while we drive for maybe a mile until I see a green sign lit up in the halogen headlamps. The white lettering on the sign says, TEXT STOP, ONE MILE. That's the big thing in New York State these days: Text stops, so you don't text while you're driving and end up killing yourself or worse, someone else. I need information on how to get to Perez before he can kill my family. The wounded kid in back is one of Perez's men. He will give me the information I need even if I have to torture him.

I'm gripping the wheel so tightly I feel like the bones in my fingers are about to break. When the exit for the TEXT STOP appears, I hook a right and turn onto it. The place is pretty much deserted. No cars, no big semis. But that doesn't mean somebody might not pull in at any second. I need to work fast.

I put the stick in park, leave the engine running. Grabbing my gun, I open the door, get out. Opening the backseat door, I lean in, place the gun barrel against the gangster's tattooed head. He squirms, mumbles something into the duct tape. He's trying desperately to free his legs and hands, but he's not even close to strong enough. A puddle of blood has gathered on the leather seat.

Reaching inside with my free hand, I slide my fingers into the back pocket on his baggy jeans, pull out a black leather wallet. Opening the wallet, I see a New York State Driver's license. In the picture, he's smiling. He's maybe a couple years younger than he is now and he's got a full head of thick black hair. I'll be damned if he isn't the spitting image of a young Don Juan.

The date of birth on the license is 03/03/2001. What's that make him? Early twenties? I see the name. Juan Enrico Perez, Junior. He's a junior, just like my Bradley.

"Jesus," I say to myself. "It's got to be Don Juan's son. I had no idea he even had a son."

I toss the wallet. Taking hold of the arm that's attached to the injured shoulder, I cock it back a little. The kid winces in pain, his eyes rolling back in their sockets.

"Are you Don Juan's son?" I beg.

He can't speak with the tape wrapped around his mouth, so I tell him to nod his head for yes, shake his head for no.

"Got it?" I add.

He nods. Good. The kid is willing to cooperate.

"Are you Don Juan Perez's son?" I repeat.

His eyes are wide and dilated. I can't help but wonder if he's high on something. Crack maybe. Meth. Bubble Gum. Or maybe it's just the result of his pain, and his bleeding out all over Sean's Volkswagen interior.

He nods, slowly.

"Oh fuck," I whisper to myself.

"Oh my God," Joanne says, speaking up finally. "I didn't know Juan had a son either. Maybe he has a million of them."

"So, you really are Don Juan's son," I say while shooting her a quick look. Then, yanking his arm a little more, watching the kid squirm. "Jeeze, he must be real proud of you, gangbanger."

Another nod. Once more, I glance at Joanne. She's staring at the kid, not with sadness or empathy for his pain, but pure hatred.

"Ask him if he's the one who shot our Bradley," she insists, not only pointing her pistol at him, but cocking back the hammer like she's Dirty Harry.

I turn back to him.

"You heard the lady," I say through clenched teeth.

I give him a poke in the bad shoulder with my pistol barrel. He winces again, a big tear falling from his left eye. He's not saying anything. Okay, that's not right. What I mean is, he's not nodding his head. Or shaking it. He's just looking up at me with those wide, cloudy eyes. That's when something dawns on me. This kid…this gangster, this drug runner, this murderer…is afraid of me. He's afraid of *us*. I've never before experienced anyone who's been afraid of me. Not even Martin was afraid of me, until I stood up for myself and punched him. Until we killed him.

I'm looking into the eyes of Don Juan Perez's son, and I can't help but feel good. I feel powerful. The son of one of this world's most powerful drug cartel members is afraid of me. He's afraid of my wife.

"Did…you…shoot...our…son?" I ask, poking him once with the pistol barrel with each word uttered.

He not only winces in pain. He convulses. This time, big tears fall from both eyes.

Finally, he manages to work up a slow nod. The rage swims through my veins like hot acid. I gaze at Joanne, see her face go so tight I'm afraid her skin might split down the center. She brings the pistol barrel closer to his face. The kid closes his eyes like he knows he's about to get it right between the eyes.

"Not yet, Joanne!" I shout. "We need the son of bitch alive for a few more minutes."

"Why?!" she spits.

She's also crying. But these are not tears of fear or sadness. They are tears of anger, hatred, frustration.

"We need him alive to get our son and your mother back. You understand?"

Shoving my gun back into my pant waist, I pull out my camera once more. I go to the text app, thumb on the text thread with Don Juan. Aiming the phone at Juan Junior's face, I snap a couple of pictures and then press send.

Inhaling a breath, I type, "I see we both have something in common. We both have Juniors."

I stare at the text thread. The pictures of Juan Junior look brutal. His shoulder is bleeding badly. His eyes are wide, frightened, his face so pale the tattoos that cover his head seem to stick out like three dimensional objects. The swastika branded on his skull cap sits beside a depiction of Jesus, His head wrapped in a crown of thorns while, His desperate eyes stare up at a heaven that might not exist…It all gives me a sick feeling.

"What did he say?" Joanne asks.

"Hang on," I say.

A text comes back. I open it.

It says, "You are in over your head, gringo." Then another text. "Speaking of heads…"

"What's he saying, Bradly? Joanne presses.

Something's happening at the Don Juan downtown fortress, and I don't like it. Something's happening to Bradley Junior, or Joanne's mother. My gut is telling me that Don Juan won't take our holding his wounded son hostage, lightly. But then, he won't take a chance on harming our loved ones with his last remaining son under our control. Or would he?

Speaking of heads…

What the hell is that supposed to mean?

Another text. This time, a photo comes through. What I see makes everything in my stomach come up on me. I jump out of the car, phone in hand, and puke my guts onto the blacktop.

"Bradley, what the hell is wrong?!" Joanne shouts from inside the car. "What is going on?! What's making you sick?!"

Standing, I take another look at the picture. Joanne's mother's head is sitting in her lap. One of Don Juan's men is standing beside her. He's bare chested, his head shaved, and just like all the others, he's covered in tattoos. He's got a bolo gripped in his right hand, and he's got a wide smile on his face. He's decapitated Joanne's mother.

What the hell do I do now? Do I tell her the truth? That her mother has been murdered? That her head has been cut off? If I tell her the truth, she will shoot Don Juan's son on the spot, and then Don Juan will kill Bradley Junior. She gets out of the car, comes around the front, stomps over to me. Her face is so full of fear and anger, it's like I'm not looking at my wife anymore. She's crying again, and she's shaking. She's got the gun gripped tightly in her hand and her hands are trembling.

"Tell…me…what the fuck is wrong, Bradley!" she screams.

I try to open my mouth, try to make the words come out, but I can't.

"Is it Bradley Junior?" she begs. "Have they killed him?"

I shake my head, and stare at her through eyes that also fill with tears. She takes another step forward.

"Then it's got to be my mother," she says, her voice hoarse and coming from a deep, dark place inside her soul.

"Joanne," I say. "I'm sorry."

She takes another step forward.

"Let me see it," she insists. "He sent you something. A picture. Let…me…see…it!"

"Joanne," I say. "You don't want to see this. Trust me, you don't want to look at it."

Raising the gun, she aims the barrel at me.

"I swear to God as my judge, Bradley Jones," she says, "I will shoot your fucking head off if you don't show me your phone."

My God, this is what it's all come down to. For the second time in one night, my wife is aiming a loaded gun at me and for the second time tonight someone close to Joanne has been ruthlessly murdered. What the hell has happened to us? To our lives? We've become monsters and in the end, monsters always answer to the devil.

Slowly, almost achingly, I turn the phone around, and show her the screen. When she's finally able to focus on the photo, her knees buckle, and she drops to the pavement like a sack of rags and bones. She's not passed out, but instead, entirely broken down. She's weeping so hard, she can hardly breathe.

I drop to my knees, try to take her in my arms. But she's fighting me, punching me with clenched fists.

"Joanne, calm down," I plead. "Perez is a monster."

She punches me again in the chest, then pushes herself off me. That's when she stands. Gun in hand, she starts approaching the car. I see then that the kid's torso is hanging out of the backseat. He's trying to escape. Joanne raises the pistol and takes aim.

I shoot back up onto my feet.

"Joanne!" I scream. "Don't do it!"

I run to her, grab her arm. A shot is fired. The bullet is way off its mark. Taking hold of her arm, I grab the gun, snatch it out of her hand.

"What are you doing?!" she screams. "He deserves to die for what Perez did to my mother! For shooting our son! For killing Sean!"

She's squirming, trying her hardest to free herself from my grip.

"I know," I say. "You're right. He deserves to die. But not yet. Don't you see, Joanne? We need him alive to make an exchange for our son. If we kill him now, then Bradley is as good as dead. But if we keep him alive, then Don Juan has no choice but to keep Bradley alive."

She calms down as the words sink in. She's breathing heavily, her face wet with tears. Finally, I let her go, and she looks up at the cloud-filled night, as if silently cursing God. Lowering her head, she looks me in the eyes.

"You do what you have to do, Bradley," she says. "But mark my word, before tomorrow is through, I will kill Juan Perez *and* his son, if it's the last thing I do."

She walks away from me, goes to Juan Junior and starts shoving him back in the Volkswagen. But not before turning back to me.

"And if Bradley Junior dies," she says, "I will kill you too."

10

Another text comes through. My heart pumps wildly when I see that it's from Don Juan. I open it.

"Now our leverage is equal. Is it not, amigo?"

"I'm not your friend," I text in return, wiping the rainwater from the screen.

The phone rings then. It's him. No more texting. I bring the phone to my ear.

"Yeah," I say with a dry mouth and racing pulse.

"It seems we have reached an impasse you and me, gringo," he says, with all the coolness and calmness of a surgeon. "You see, the old lady, she had to go. She was creating an imbalance in leverage. Now you have my son, and I have your son, and our leverage is balanced."

Swallowing a deep, bitter breath. "So how do we play this, you and I, Don Juan?"

"That all depends on what you want?"

"I just want my son back, alive," I say. "I don't give a fuck that you stole our cookers and that you're working directly with Carcov. I don't give a rat's ass about making Bubble Gum anymore. I don't care about any of it. I just want my son back and to be left alone for the rest of my life."

"Such a noble man," he says. "But let me tell you something, gringo, once you're in the drug trade there is no getting out unless you plan on going to the police. How do I know you're not standing right beside Detective Danish right this very moment?"

"You don't," I say.

He laughs. It's a deep, mocking laugh. I wipe the rain from my eyes with the back of my hand.

"Well, I'll tell you what I will do for you," he says. "I will agree to meet you, face to face, in a place we both agree upon. There, we will make the safe exchange of our sons. Que?"

A face to face with Don Juan. It's exactly what I was hoping for.

"Some place out in the open," I say. "No traps, no ambushes. Is that clear?"

"If you're asking me if I agree with you, I do," he says. "I know of such a place across the river from the city. It's an old fuels factory that was abandoned long ago. It's now just a wasteland of old pipes and busted up brick factory buildings. Meet me in the big parking lot in the center of the facility at noon tomorrow."

"High noon," I say.

“Gary Cooper,” he says. “One of my favorites. Tell me, gringo, do you like old westerns?”

For a split second it dawns on me that I’ve spent a lot of my adult life watching old Westerns from the 1940’s, 50’s and 60s on the TV every weekend, drinking beers and getting softer and softer.

“Yeah,” I say, “I like the Spaghetti Westerns.”

“Ahhh, the great Clint Eastwood,” he says. “The good, the Bad, and The Ugly. I guess that’s what we have here. Our sons are the good, we are the bad, and what’s happened to your mother-in-law, that is the ugly, is it not?” He hesitates a bit, then laughs once more. “Perhaps I did you a favor in getting rid of her!” he barks.

“Are we done, Don Juan?” I say.

“We are done,” he says. “Oh, and Gringo, I’m sure I don’t have to tell you that should my son die, your boy will receive the same fate as grandma.”

I swallow a mouthful of dry bitterness once more and feel a chill run through my rain-soaked body.

“High noon,” he repeats.

Then he cuts the connection.

Heading back to the car, I assist an equally soaked Joanne with pushing Juan Junior back into the car. The rain has started back up again, and my shirt and head are soaked by the time I set myself back behind the wheel. Joanne produces a handkerchief from her bag.

“Here,” she says, handing it to me. “Dry yourself off before you catch cold.”

She still cares…

I turn the wipers back on high and wipe my face and head. In the back seat, the kid is moaning through his tape.

"We need to get him some medical care," Joanne says, "or the worst could happen. Not that I wouldn't like to watch every minute of it."

"I know," I say, pulling back on the highway. "But we need a few more things first. We gotta head back to Catskill. Then we'll grab some food and some medical supplies at a drug store. That's the best we can do for him."

Driving, I pull off the next exit, then get back on the highway, southbound. When we come to the Catskill exit a few miles later, I pull off, and head straight for the hardware/general store where I bought the duct tape earlier tonight. Scratch that, where I bought the duct tape last night I should say, since it's going on one in the morning.

I don't pull up in front of the store, but instead kill the lights and pull around back.

"You're going to break in?" Joanne says. "You sure that's a good idea?"

I give her a look.

"I think at this point, breaking and entering will be the least of our concerns." Reaching into her bag, I pull out the rest of the cash stack that I cut into when I paid for the hotel room. "And don't worry, I'm not about to steal anything. I'm going to pay for it." Holding up money. "Cash on the barrelhead."

Getting out, I shove the cash into my pocket. I go to the back door, wrap my hand around the doorknob on the metal door. Of course, it's locked. I look around. Beside the dumpster, I see a couple concrete blocks and other assorted debris. I go to the dumpster, pick up one of the blocks, bring it with me back to the door. Using both hands I raise the block up, then bring it down hard and fast onto the doorknob. It snaps right off. Dropping the block, I stuff my fingertips into the now exposed round hole, pull the demolished lock out, and yank the door open.

The place is dark, and I don't feel like turning on a light and attracting a cop. But there's enough light from the streetlamps spilling through the big front glass windows for me to see, once my eyes adjust, that is. I head to the front counter, grab a plastic bag, then set out to grab what I need. A small one-foot length of PVC pipe, a couple end caps, a pile of nails, some crucial chemicals from the muzzle loader section, a set of walkie talkies, a small relay kit that's also available next to the radios, and a few more assorted goodies. I then head to the gunracks and pull an AR15 off the wall. Setting that on the front counter, I go back to the gunrack and stuff three boxes of .288 ammo into my bag. By now, the bag is stuffed.

Heading back to the counter once more, I set the bag on top then reach into my pocket for the cash. The AR15 is eight hundred bucks alone, plus the cost of all other stuff. I peel off two thousand five hundred dollars and set it on the counter. That will cover the cost of the damages to the back door plus the merchandise, and still leave the old man a nice little tip for his troubles. I exit the store the same way I came in.

Opening the hatch back, I set everything inside. Then, I get back behind the wheel.

"It's been a while since I spent any time in Catskill," I say, "but if I remember correctly, there's a twenty-four-hour Duane Reade right down the road across from a strip mall. There's a

Dunkin Donut too that might be open all night. I'll head in the Duane Reade and you can get us some coffee and donuts or whatever."

Pulling out of the hardware store lot, I drive in the direction of the drug store, while I silently pray we don't run into a state trooper road block. The rain has stopped again, so I don't bother with the wipers. When I see the brightly lit signage for the Duane Reade, I pull in and park deep into the lot so we can't be seen from the road. Killing the engine, I get out.

"The Dunkin Donut is across the street," I say.

"What about him," Joanne says, gesturing towards the back.

I steal a quick look at the kid.

"He's passed out, snoring up a storm," I say. "In his condition, he's going nowhere. Besides, I'll be two minutes. I'll pick you up outside the Dunkin Donut."

She nods. I open the door, get out and head to the drug store entrance. Once inside, I go straight to the First Aid aisle. I'm quick and consciously keeping my head down since for certain the CCTV here works just fine, no doubt. I grab some gauze, a brown bottle of peroxide, and some surgical tape. I could grab some pain killers too, but that would just make things too comfortable for the kid who tried to kill my kid.

I bring it all up to the counter. A college age young man with earbuds in his ear holes looks at me suspiciously. He reminds me of the young guy who worked at the Lowes back when I had to buy all the ingredients necessary for dissolving two human bodies. My gut tells me he's going to ask me something about my purchases. He picks up the bottle of peroxide, scans it.

"Everything okay at home, dude?" he asks.

There it is. Exactly what I knew was going to happen.

“Not really,” I say. “Why else would I be shopping at the Duane Reade at one in the morning?”

“Hope nobody’s hurt bad,” he goes on.

“Thanks,” I say. Then, “And if you ask me anymore nosy questions about my purchases, I’ll knock your teeth down your throat.”

His face goes pale. His lower lip trembles.

“Sorry,” he says.

He rings it all up. I pay cash. He gives me my change. For a quick second or two, I leave feeling really good over the fact that people are afraid of me these days.

Back in the car, I open the back door, and seat myself beside the kid. I tear open one of the gauze bandages, and soak it in some peroxide. Then, tearing away his wife beater, I apply it to the entry wound. The kid is still passed out, but he definitely feels the sting, because he squirms and makes just the slightest hint of a high-pitched cry. I then tear off a couple of pieces of tape and attach the bandage to his shoulder. I pull him forward and repeat the process with the exit wound. He squirms and cries then too, but somehow remains passed out. It’s then I realize that without real medical help the kid could die sooner than later. His blood is smeared all over the back seat. Lots of it. High noon can’t come soon enough.

Going back around the front of the car, I get back behind the wheel, and start the engine. Sirens coming from out of the near distance raise the fine hairs on the back of my neck. Police sirens. Did the nosy young man who rang me out at the Duane Reade call the cops? I’m not about to wait around to find out. Speeding out of the parking lot, I cross the road and enter the Dunkin' Donuts lot. Joanne is standing outside the building with coffees and a bag of donuts in hand.

Leaning over the center console, I open the door for her.

"Get in quick," I say.

She leans in, sets the coffees into the two cup holders, then sets herself in the shotgun seat. I pull away as she's closing the door.

"What's wrong?" she asks.

"You hear those sirens, Jo?"

"No," she says.

"You will in a second."

I pull around the back of the donut shop and stop. When the sirens get really loud, I know the cops are only a few dozen feet away.

"Now I hear them," she says.

"I think the guy who rang me out inside the drug store called the cops," I say.

Pulling a little more forward, I see two state trooper cruisers drive into the Duane Reade parking lot.

"I hate it when I'm right," I say.

"Let's just get the hell out of here, Brad."

"You only gotta tell me once."

Minutes later, we're back on the highway, speeding our way towards Albany. While I sip on my coffee, Joanne tries to get the kid to eat a donut, but he's too groggy from blood loss, and he shoves her away. At least he's still alive. For what it's worth, I have no appetite either, but I shove down a blueberry cake donut just for the sugar rush. At least that, plus the coffee is keeping me alert.

I've finished with the coffee by the time the lights from the city are visible on the horizon. Joanne is fast asleep, and I don't dare wake her. Come sunup, she'll need every ounce of energy she's got for what I have planned. I don't dare drive to our Hope Street home, but instead, head directly for the old King Fuels facility. It's located under a big metal bridge that spans the Hudson River and connects the old city of Troy to Albany. Driving down into the old wasteland of a fuel refinery, it's like entering another world.

To my right are crumbling old brick buildings that must have been state of the art in the late 1800s. But now the three and four-story structures have succumbed to the ravages of time, and they look like something out of Berlin, circa 1945. To my left is what's left of the refinery. Just a pile of massive metal pipes intertwined in and around a big black tank. Next to that is another series of what look like bombed out brick buildings. A gravel parking lot occupies the center of the dystopian setting. It reminds me of Armageddon itself. A place that might have served as the setting for the Mad Max flicks back in the 1980s.

As I slowly pull into the gravel lot, the Volkswagen LED headlamps cause the eyes on a couple coy dogs to light up in the darkness. They bark and run away, one of them with what looks like a squirrel trapped in its jaws. I don't dare leave the car in the lot but instead, back it up in between two adjoining brick buildings. Killing the engine, I lock the doors, and lean the seat back just a little. Resting my head against the seatback, I'm out like a broken light.

11

I wake with a start, the bright early Fall sun shining down through the windshield. But it doesn't feel like early Fall. More like mid-July. My body is sweating and baking in the sun. Gaze at the time. Nine AM. Holy shit, we've been out for hours. I nudge Joanne. She also wakes with a start.

"What time is it?" she asks groggily.

I tell her.

"That late?" she says. Then, eyeing me. "You think he's still alive?"

"Let's hope so."

Undoing her seatbelt, she spins around in her seat, extends her arm, brings the tips of her fingers to the kid's jugular. She presses them there for a bit. When she turns to me and nods, I feel a shot of relief swim through my veins.

"Should we change his dressing?" Joanne asks.

“His father will be here in three hours,” I say. “Let him change it.” Then, opening the door. “You and I have some work to do.”

Getting out, I go around the car to the hatch back with the shattered glass. I open it. Joanne also gets out, stretches herself. Pulling out the AR15, I thumb the magazine release, allow the empty mag to drop into my hand.

“You already know how to use this, Jo,” I say. “But a little refresher might be in order.”

She grabs the long gun from me, pulls back the bolt, then releases it. She shoulders the weapon, aims at nothing in particular, and dry fires.

“Sean might have been more trouble than he was worth,” she says, “but he was a good gun coach.”

I don’t bother with responding to her observation since I still can’t quite shake the image of my old friend T-boning my wife in the basement. That said, we spend the next hour making plans for where Joanne is going to position herself with the AR15 so she can be of maximum use against what is surely going to be an army accompanying Don Juan Perez.

Joanne is more than familiar with the weapon. I also know how to work one, again thanks to Sean, may he rest in peace, regardless of his screwing around with my wife. It’s something I have got to put out of my mind for now...maybe forever. There’s just too much at stake in the form of our son, and our future as free people. In a word, prison is not an option.

Once we’ve settled on our plan of action, Joanne and I get back in the car, pull out of the abandoned King Fuels facility and head to the nearest stop n’ rob for a coffee, and a quick wash. No one feels like eating anything, but we do buy some bottled water. We make the stop quick, parking way off to the side behind the dumpster, and take turns going inside the store, so that Juan Jr. doesn't get away. That is, he wakes up. I'm also praying no one has the chance to recognize us or get a good look at the shot-up kid seated in the backseat. Like I said, the back window is shot out. That alone is enough to attract unwanted attention.

On the way back to King Fuels, I tune into the local Spectrum 24 Hour News. One of the leading stories is about the shootings that took place at the Riviera Motel in Catskill and the subsequent drive-by shooting and possible quadruple homicide of four suspected drug cartel gang members. Once again, Detective David Danish has been placed in charge of delivering a presser about the events.

"Last night, at approximately eleven o'clock, a gang of four Latino drug cartel members shot up a Catskill motel room that was apparently rented by Bradley Jones, his wife Joanne, and one, Sean MacDonald, 58, of North Albany. MacDonald, who was a business partner of the Jones', was found dead at the scene of an apparent gunshot wound to the head. The Jones were not found at the scene. They and any possessions they had with them were gone, telling me they were able to escape the fusillade of automatic and semi-automatic gunfire."

I picture the dapper Danish, standing at a podium outside the South Pearl Street Precinct. He's clean shaven, maybe dressed in a blue blazer and tan khakis. The attractive young lady reporter, along with a dozen other young reporters hungry for a scoop, will be holding their smartphones in his direction to catch his every word.

"Later that night, sometime around midnight," Danish goes on, "the black Chevy Suburban that was being driven by the four gang members was discovered shot up at an intersection between Route 9W and Farmers Road just north of the town of Catskill. Three of the gang members were found to be deceased, while the driver was missing from the scene, telling me he either survived the shooting or was purposely abducted by whoever did the shooting."

"Were the shooters the Jones?" the pretty woman asks. At least, I think that's her voice.

"Obviously, we don't know that for a fact," Danish says. "But right now, that's our suspicion."

"Who was the driver?" a man interjects.

"We're not sure at this point," Danish says. "But we're pretty confident he, and the other three, work for Juan Perez."

"Why hasn't Juan Perez been arrested yet?" someone else asks.

"Ask the FBI that question," Danish answers bitterly.

"How close are you to finding the Jones and is this an all-out drug war in Upstate New York?"

"Where is Doctor Bradley Jones Junior?" a third person barks. "We understand he's been removed from the Albany Medical Center. Rumors abound he was abducted by Perez, right from under the APD's noses."

"I can't speculate on any of that at this time," Danish says, his voice sounding annoyed. "That's it for now. Thank you all."

With that, Danish leaves the platform. Or so I assume. I turn the radio off, as we re-enter the old entrance to King Fuels.

"No word about our son," Joanne says, sipping her coffee. "No word about my mother going missing from the home."

"I wonder why Danish is keeping all that quiet," I say. "I can't speak to your mother's situation at the elderly facility. But Danish has got to know our boy was kidnapped from the hospital by Perez."

"Maybe he's too embarrassed to say anything to the press about it," Joanne surmises. "Maybe he was in charge."

I give her a quick glance as we pass by the broken-down old brick buildings on one side, and the big old black fuel tank on the other. I glance at my watch. It's a little past eleven. Soon, Perez and his men will be arriving along with our son. I *pray* they will be arriving with my son, that is. Both Joanne's and my phone are out of power now, and we can't plug in our wall chargers since we left them in the shot-up motel room. So, it's not like we can make contact with Don Juan and remind him to bring our son to us, like he promised.

I don't park the car in between the buildings like I did last night, but instead in the middle of the lot. I also turn the car around, facing the exit just in case we need to make a speedy escape.

"So now we just wait?" Joanne says.

"Grab your AR, and head to the spot we chose," I say. "When the time comes for you to enact our plan, I will give you a hand signal. Understand?"

"Enact our plan," she says. "Hand signal." Then, "Mind if I bring my coffee, Brad?"

"Knock yourself out."

She gets out, goes around to the hatchback, doesn't bother with opening it, but instead reaches into the broken window and once more pulls out the AR15. She heads towards one of the two, four-story brick buildings where she's to set up a perch inside a shattered window on the fourth floor. From there, she'll have perfect, unobstructed shooting. As for me, I get out, open the backseat door, check for a pulse on young Juan. His heart is still beating, but his pulse is faint. He's also pissed himself. This thing can't end soon enough.

Going to the hatchback, I open it. Pulling out Sean's 9mm, I drop the magazine into my hand. I refill it with rounds, add one more for the chamber, and slap the mag back home. The spare magazine in my pocket is still full. Placing the gun in my pant waist, I grab hold of the length of plastic pipe, and proceed to do what I have to do with it. When the project is completed, I grab hold of the radio relay, and take care of business. You might find me a little vague here, but any more information at this point would be TMI.

Setting everything neatly back in the plastic bag, I then close the hatchback and once more, check my watch. Five minutes until high noon. Going around the front of the car, I look up at the nearest building's fourth floor. I see Joanne. She gives me a wave. She also does something that takes me a little by surprise, but that also makes me feel good. And feeling good is something I haven't done in a long, long time. She blows me a kiss, just like she used to do when we were college kids.

Don Juan has got to be on his way. My pulse is pounding, and my mouth is dry, the adrenaline in my brain heating up and making my temples pound like tympani. But I'm also feeling a warm, wonderful sensation swim through my body. Joanne still loves me, and I still love her. No matter what happened with Sean, it doesn't matter. I still love her. We're different people now than we were when we first fell for one another all those decades ago, but the love has somehow stayed the same. Now all we need to be whole again is to get our son back, alive.

Then, coming from behind me, the sound of engines. Big engines. Turning, I see two big black Suburbans coming towards us along the dusty, Indian Summer sunbaked, gravel road. Our high noon showdown with Donn Juan Perez is about to begin.

12

One of the Suburbans comes to a stop maybe one hundred feet in front of me, while the other speeds past me and comes to a stop maybe fifty feet behind my position. Obviously, Perez plans on making sure I have no chance of getting away. He's got me trapped. But what he doesn't realize, is that it's something I thought out, or hoped for anyway. It's certainly something Joanne anticipated since she's seen this kind of thing a hundred times before from watching Netflix. In a word, I couldn't have asked for a more perfect setup.

I feel Joanne's eyes on me, waiting for the right time to give her the signal. I also place my shooting hand on the grip of the 9mm. The doors open on both SUVs. Four men get out behind me and four emerge before me. All of them gangsters, and parodies of themselves. Shaved heads, faces and necks covered in colorful tattoos of Jesus and swastikas and God knows what else. They're all packing automatic long guns. M16s by the looks of them.

The only different looking one in the bunch is Don Juan Perez. He's wearing an expensive blue suit, the ball knot on his matching red and white striped rep tie executed perfectly. Like myself, he's packing a 9mm semi-automatic handgun. Since he could easily have the jump on me, I decide to draw mine from my waist, while keeping the barrel aimed at the ground. But that one little move causes all the gangsters to quickly shoulder their weapons. The mechanical noise of their weapons being cocked reverberates across the empty lot.

"How is my boy, Gringo?" Don Juan asks.

The sun is shining down on us. It's too hot for early Fall and the heat is rising off the gravel surface in the near distance as an eerie haze. The breeze picks up the dust, and makes small funnel clouds out of it, like little tornados.

"I was just about to ask you the same thing, Don Juan."

Taking a step forward, Perez forms a wide smile.

"How do I know if he is alive if I can't see him?"

"You'll have to take my word for it," I say. "But he could use a hospital, and soon."

His smile fades, and he spits onto the gravel floor.

"How is *my* son?" I ask.

"He's alive," Don Juan says. "Just know this, Gringo. He too can use a hospital." He starts to laugh then. "You know, this is quite the situation we're in. It's kind of like the duel at the end of For a Few Dollars More. When the professional gunfighter faces down the amateur, and the great Clint Eastwood looks on, knowing precisely who is going to be the victor."

"And who would that be, Don Juan?" I say.

He spits and laughs again. He also takes yet another step forward.

“You can’t win, Gringo,” he says. “You are outgunned. Outmanned. And dare I say it, outsmarted. You have always been and always will be an amateur. When you decided to get into this business after killing my brothers, you got in over your head. You had no idea who you were dealing with, even if you did get lucky with creating a spectacular product which I now own. Me, I am a professional who could have killed you long ago. But I felt sorry for you. You are simply a mailman, and your wife, she is a just a wife. A homemaker, I believe you call them. A Betty fucking Crocker. To be honest, you remind me of my mama and papa. You are simple people who are caught up in a very extraordinary and dangerous situation. And now you will die if you don’t give me my son back…alive.”

There comes a long pause where silence fills the abandoned King Fuels plant. It’s not really a silence since way off in the distance you can make out the sound of trucks and vehicles driving over the bridge. There’s also the buzz of insects and cicadas. I look into the eyes of the gangsters who want to shoot me to bits. I feel the eyes of the ones behind me. If I were a betting man, I’d wager that Joanne and I aren’t making it out of here alive. That killing us…all of us…has been Don Juan’s plan all along. That is, unless we can kill them first.

“You haven’t asked about her,” I say after a time.

“Excuse me, Gringo?” Don Juan asks.

“You haven’t said a word about, Joanne,” I say, “other than referring to her as Betty fucking Crocker.”

He smiles again, almost warmly.

“Why, of course,” he says. “I pray she is still among us. She may be a simple woman, but she is so very pretty. Is she still alive?”

"Oh," I say while slowly raising my free hand, "she's alive all right. In fact, she's right here."

Dropping my free hand fast, like the flagman at a raceway, I give Joanne the signal. That's when I hit the dirt. She shoots rapid fire at the four gangsters behind me, while I slip under the Volkswagen. All seven gangsters open up full-automatic fire. Turning myself so I get a quick look at the gangsters behind me, I see they are concentrating their fire up at the brick building's fourth floor. But Joanne has already picked off one of them. The hit gangster now lies flat on his belly, bleeding out from a head wound the size of a lemon.

Turning towards Perez, I see that the three gangsters with him are directing their fire at me. But instead of hitting me, they're hitting their own men in the crossfire. They're ripping the second Suburban to shreds. Like I said, they could not have chosen a better setup.

From down on my belly, I take aim at Don Juan's legs. He's screaming at his men to hold their fire. Inhaling a half breath, I shoot and nail the drug lord in the left shin. He drops on the spot. Scooching myself out from under the Volkswagen on the passenger side, I quickly go around the hatch back and duck for cover. Gazing over my shoulder, I see that all four gangsters behind me have been hit. They are all either badly wounded or dead, and so is their SUV. I focus on the fourth-floor window, see Joanne drop an empty magazine and immediately replace it with a fresh one. She resumes firing as if the dead gangsters aren't quite dead enough. How she manages to do this so quickly and with such skill is an amazing thing to see. For a nearsighted lady who barely drove the speed limit, she has become a crack shot. A killer.

When the four gangsters behind me have been disposed of, I shift my focus back to Perez. While I see that the drug kingpin is down for the count, writhing in pain, I can also see there's only one gangster left standing. He's got his M16 aimed at the fourth floor. But I plant a bead on his chest and pull the trigger. I score a direct hit. Joanne immediately follows up with a head shot. His body hits the gravel before the back of his skull does.

It's then the shooting stops as quickly as it began. The gunfight couldn't have taken more than fifteen or twenty seconds. We've not only managed to stay alive, but we've put down Don Juan and his entire army of gangbangers.

I come out from behind the Volkswagen. Peering into the back seat, I see that Juan Junior hasn't been hit. I can only hope my son hasn't been hit either. That is, Don Juan even brought my son along.

Footsteps coming from behind me. I turn quick.

"How's our son?" Joanne says.

I'm relieved to see she isn't wounded…that she's alive.

"That's what we're about to find out," I say while spinning around on the balls of my feet. "Isn't that right, Don Juan?!" I shout.

He's still down on the ground on his ass, his shin spurting blood, like I managed to hit not only flesh and bone but an artery. He's trying to aim his pistol at me, but I approach him anyway. When I come to him, I kick the pistol out of his hand with my booted foot. He's now entirely unarmed.

"You have no idea the hornet's nest you have kicked, Gringo," he spits.

Joanne goes to Don Juan's SUV, steps over a couple corpses, and opens the back door. Her face lights up.

“He’s alive, Bradley!” she shouts, her tears already falling. Happy tears. “Our son is okay!”

“What about my son, Gringo?” Don Juan says. “Has he been hit?”

I plant my foot on his wounded lower leg. He lets loose with a high-pitched scream.

“Before we discuss your son,” I say, “we need to discuss my wife’s and my severance package.”

He spits for a third time.

“Fuck your severance package,” he says through gritted teeth. “You don’t get no fucking severance package in our business.”

“You got our Bubble Gum, plus the assholes who cook it,” I say. “Then you must add the cold-blooded murder of our partner, and the shooting of our son. Not to mention the headaches you’ve caused us, Don Juan.”

I press harder on his shin. He squeals like a gut-shot dog.

“Fucking stop, stop, stop!” he cries.

“Oh, and then there’s the issue of Joanne’s mom,” I add. “What kind of animal does that shit to a sweet old lady, Juan? I thought Mexicans were Catholic.”

I dig my heel in, and his eyes roll up in the back of his head. He loses consciousness for a brief second or two. He’s now crying real tears, the moisture running down his face, soaking his mustache.

“Please,” he pleads. “Just take the vehicle and be on your way. I will no longer bother you if you just please leave.”

“We are going,” I say. “But I need you to do something for me. I need you to pull out your cell phone, and I need you to PayPal me.”

“PayPal you, Gringo?”

I drop to one knee.

“Phone,” I say, holding out my hand.

Slowly he reaches into his jacket pocket, pulls out an iPhone. He doesn’t type a code into it, but instead presses the pad on his index finger to the biometric security device located on the phone’s back. He slaps the phone into my hand.

“Now look at that,” I say. “Looks like you have a PayPal account. Let’s see that hand of yours again.”

“Fuck…you!”

I punch his leg.

“Okay, okay,” he spits.

I take hold of the index finger on his right hand and press the pad against the biometric device once more. That does the trick because his PayPal account opens.

“Now,” I say, “I don’t want to be greedy, but you do owe my wife and I an awful lot. Let’s say thirty…no scratch that. Forty million and we’ll call it even. Sound good to you, Don Juan?”

"You motherfucker, I will kill you for this."

"No, you won't. I can bet when the big bosses in Mexico find out about this fuck up of yours, it will be your head that'll be resting in your lap."

I go to Send Money. Then I type in my PayPal address and send myself $40Million from Don Juan's own account. I can bet he's got hundreds of millions in cash, so I feel quite confident the payment will go through. When the screen says, "You've successfully sent money," I know I'm in the clear. Just to be safe, I switch to my PayPal account, and initiate an instant transfer to Joanne's and my overseas account. It costs me $400K to do it, but it's well worth the money. Typing in my bank account info, I see that the money has been successfully transferred. That's when I go to my Coinbase Pro account, and purchase $30million in Bitcoin. As of that moment, neither the IRS, the FBI, nor any law enforcement agency the world over, can touch our money.

"Oh, and one more thing, Don Juan," I say. "You are to deliver my wife's mother to the morgue at the Albany Medical Center immediately. Her body is no good to you, so I'm sure you'll have no issue agreeing to this demand. Perhaps one of your three new employees can take care of this on your behalf since they are also experts in the death business. You know, Karl, the tall Russian, stone-faced one? He's no stranger to the morgue."

I thumb the text app on Don Juan's phone, search his contacts for a man name Karl with a K, as if I'm going through his private business Rolodex. Sure enough, I find what I'm looking for. I type, "Karl, drop what you are doing and immediately deliver Esther's body to the Albany Medical Center morgue in one of your Fitzgerald funeral home hearses."

I send the text.

"If the morgue receives a body like that one," Perez says, "they will know she's been murdered."

"I'm sure Karl will know enough to bring enough cash with him to grease the palm of anyone who cares, Don Juan. Besides, that's not my problem."

Standing, I drop the phone to the gravel. Pulling the 9mm from my waist band, I aim for the digital screen and press the trigger. The phone shatters into a million little pieces.

"That's just in case you were thinking of texting Karl back, Don Juan."

Turning, I go back to the Volkswagen, grab Joanne's bag out of the front seat. I also grab the materials from out of the hatchback and place them in her bag. I go to the driver's side, reach in the open window, pull the keys out of the ignition. Walking back to Don Juan, I toss them to the dirt near his face.

"What about my boy?" Don Juan begs.

"A deal's a deal, Hefe," I say. "You'll find Junior very much alive. But for how long, that's up to you, now isn't it?"

"Let's go Joanne," I say. "We've still got work to do."

She slips herself into the back of Don Juan's Suburban to be near our son. I open the driver's side door, get in. The vehicle isn't too badly shot up, the windshield is still intact other than a couple of bullet holes towards its center, and the keys are still in the ignition. I fire the big engine up, then adjust the seat for my long legs. Peeling out, I spray Don Juan with gravel. Making a one hundred eighty-degree turn, we head for the King Fuel's exit. As we near it, I glance into the rearview. I see the badly wounded Don Juan, fallen drug lord for the Escobar Cartel, crawling towards Sean's Volkswagen and his near-death boy.

13

First things first. We need to get Bradley Junior back in the hospital. It's exactly how I put it to Joanne.

"Can he talk, Jo?" I ask.

She asks him.

He's very weak, but he mumbles, "Yes."

He's still dressed in his hospital gown, but from what I can see of him in the rearview, it's filthy and stained with fresh blood where his gunshot wounds are located. His face is pale under his thick beard and his hair mussed up and greasy. He also looks thin, almost frail, like he hasn't had nourishment in days or weeks. But I know he's got to be in pain and in need of blood. Fresh blood.

"Listen to me, son," I say into the rearview. "Do you have a friend at the hospital…a good friend who you can trust that we can call? Someone who will take you into the ER through a back door so that we're not seen?"

He nods slowly. “Yes, my girlfriend. Jill. She’s a surgeon.”

“We need her phone number, son,” I say. “We need to find a payphone to call her. Our cell phones are out of power.”

I’m now regretting shooting Don Juan’s phone, no matter how good it felt. Maybe it would have been a better move to take it with us.

“It’s possible one of Perez’s men left their phones lying around inside the vehicle,” Joanne says. She’s gripping Bradley Junior’s hand tight.

I gaze around the front, focusing on the dash and then the center console. I don’t see any phones. I open the console. Nothing inside but some old CDs. Leaning across the passenger seat, I open the glove box. A semi-automatic is stored in there along with a couple of extra magazines. I close the glove box.

“Nothing,” I say.

“Nothing back here either,” Joanne says. “They must all be carrying their phones, not that they need them.”

“Wouldn’t have done us much good anyway, Jo,” I say. “Even if we went back to retrieve one of them, we’d never guess the phone’s passwords. We need a payphone and I know exactly where I can find one.”

Having crossed the bridge that spans the Hudson River, we’re now heading into the heart of the city. I drive Henry Johnson Boulevard until I see the same Stewarts Bread and Butter Shop where I originally placed my call to Danish about the Camps having killed the Perez brothers. Something I’m not proud of, but also something that seems like it happened forever ago. Pulling into the lot, I park directly in front of the wall-mounted payphone, put the transmission in park, and leave the engine running.

Turning around in my seat, I eye my sick son. “Can you remember her number, Brad?”

His eyes are slowly opening and closing. He looks like he’s about to pass out.

“It’s…in my…speed-dial,” he mumbles.

“Think, son,” I beg. “Think real hard. You don’t have your phone.”

He nods again.

Inhaling and exhaling, he slowly reveals a number. I repeat it for him. He nods again. Opening the door, I get out. Digging in my pocket, I find some change. A couple quarters are mixed in with the change. But just as I’m walking to the phone, a young man comes out of nowhere, picks up the receiver and starts digging in his pocket. He’s a young white kid wearing a black hoodie.

“I need that phone,” I say.

He gives me a dirty look. I wrap my hand around a portion of the phone his small hand doesn’t cover.

“Hey, bitch,” he says. “I’m using the phone. You’re just gonna have to wait.”

I don’t hesitate to do what I have to do. Reaching into my pant waist, I pull out my semi-automatic, shove the barrel in his gut.

“My friends Smith and Wesson say otherwise…*bitch*,” I say.

He releases the phone, backs away from me. He's got his hands raised like he's trying to surrender.

"Jeeze," he says. "Take it easy, mister."

"Now go the fuck away," I say, "before I shoot you in the face."

Turning, he runs away. Replacing the gun into my pant waist, I pull out a quarter and slip it into the coin slot. I listen to the mechanical sound of the quarter falling through the phone's metal insides until it hits the cash well. That's when I get a dial-tone. Dialing Jennifer's number, I say a silent prayer to the good Lord that she'll pick up even if she doesn't recognize the number.

The connection made, the phone rings. And rings.

"Come on, come on," I say, my eyes focused on the SUV windshield.

I can barely make out my family inside it, but I know they must be eyeing me intently. They are all I have left in the world. Out the corner of my eye, I see an APD blue and white slowly pass by the store. The cop inside it eyes the big black SUV. This isn't the best section of town, so my guess is he's suspicious over an expensive ride parked at the stop n' rob. I immediately about-face.

More rings. Then, I'm directed to a voicemail.

"Oh, for fuck's sake," I say aloud.

"Hi, this is Jill," a sweet young female voice says. "I can't come to the phone right now since I'm probably trying to save someone's life. But if you leave a nice message and your phone number, I'll try and get back to you ASAP." She says ASAP like it's a real word.

I can't help but grin over her witty message, despite the dire circumstances.

Clearing my throat, "Hi Jill, my name is Bradley Jones. Brad's dad. I'm sure you know by now that he's been taken from the hospital where he badly needs to be. But we have him back and we really need to get him into the Emergency Room or ICU or wherever you need to put him to get better. Problem is, we're going to need your help. My wife and I are in a little bit of trouble and if we just show up at the hospital, the police will be notified. I'm at a payphone. Here's the number." I recite it for her. "If I don't hear from you in a few minutes, I will try and call you back. This is a matter of life and death, Jill. Please call."

I hang up. Turning, I look out for the cop. He seems to have driven on, which is my good luck. Or maybe he's spotted me and waiting for backup somewhere.

"Ring, damnit," I say aloud, as if this is going to make Jill call back any faster.

I go to the SUV, open the back door. My son looks paler than ever, the blood stains on his hospital gown growing larger, darker. He's also fully passed out. The look on my wife's face is grave.

"We need to do something now, Bradley," she says, her tone on the verge of panic. "Or he's not going to make it."

"God knows I'm trying, Jo," I say.

The payphone rings. My heart jumps into my mouth. Sprinting to the phone, I grab the receiver off the hook, press it against my ear.

"Hello," I say. "Hello."

"Hello," a woman says. "Is this Mr. Jones?"

“Jill?” I ask.

“Yes. I got your message. I’m so happy he’s still alive.” Her voice is tense, but I sense her relief over the connection.

“Alive barely,” I say. “That’s why we need your help.”

“I understand,” she says. “You’re all over the news. So is Bradley…his being shot and his going missing. Now they’re saying Mrs. Jones’s mother was kidnapped from her elderly care facility. If you don’t mind my asking, just what the heck is going on?”

“It’s true,” I say. “Mrs. Jones’s mom was kidnapped by some very bad people. The same bad people we’ve unfortunately become associated with, Jill. But believe me when I say Mrs. Jones and I are *not* bad people. We’ve made some mistakes but we’re not bad at all. We’re actually pretty average everyday folks. Until recently, that is. But I don’t have time to explain everything right now. We just need to get Bradley to the hospital and do it now before he bleeds out.”

“Okay, okay,” she says anxiously, but hesitantly at the same time. Like she’s afraid if she helps us, that makes her a co-conspirator in our… let’s call them, gross illegalities.

“Tell you what, Jill,” I go on. “Just tell us where to leave him at The Albany Medical Center and at what time, and we will drop him off. You don’t even have to see us. All you will see is Bradley. Does that work for you?”

“Yes, okay,” she says, sudden relief in her voice. She pauses for a beat. I’m assuming she’s thinking things out. “Listen, Mr. Jones, there’s an employee’s entrance around the back of the Medical Center, next to the morgue. Almost nobody uses it because it's just a lot easier to enter through the front door. Can you drop him there in forty minutes?"

I gaze at my watch. It's after one already.

"Can it be sooner? He's bleeding real bad."

"I'm all the way out in Saratoga, twenty miles away. I can't possibly be there any earlier. Just keep applying pressure to his wounds and drop him at the employee's entrance no later than two thirty. Will that work?"

"Got it, Jill," I say. "And thank you."

"I'm just glad your son is found and that he is alive."

"Me too."

"I've got to be going," she says.

"Jill," I say.

"Yes," she says like a question.

"Bradley Junior," I say. "I've never seen him this happy with a lady. He thinks the world of you."

"Well, Mr. Jones, you should know, I love him dearly. And I'm so, so relieved he's alive."

I can tell she's starting to cry as she hangs up. But then, I can't help but grin warmly.

14

Back behind the wheel of the Suburban, I relay the plan to Joanne.

"Forty minutes from now," she says with a shake of her head. "He needs to be there *now*, Bradley."

"It's the earliest she can be there," I say. "And I believe her. She's all the way up in Saratoga. Just keep applying pressure to his wounds."

My wife's hands are stained with blood from doing just that. My guess is she felt as though just holding his hand wasn't enough.

"What do we do in the meantime?" Joanne asks.

"We take a fly by to an old friend's house," I say. "Case the joint, so to speak."

"What old friend?"

"Mr. Don Juan Perez."

Backing out of the parking spot, I pull ahead, out of the lot, and onto Henry Johnson Boulevard. Perez's inner-city mansion, or should I say fortress, is located further up on the corner of Lark and Dove Streets more towards the city center. It's a massive five-story century old brick building that takes up nearly an entire city block. It's more like an arsenal than a house. Armed guards are usually perched outside, and the place is always teaming with gangsters like the ones we killed today at high noon.

It's amazing to me Don Juan has escaped arrest thus far, but his claim to be a legal importer/exporter must somehow be rock solid. If only the police could see what he's cooking in the basement of that big brick castle, they'd know the truth. But that would take a warrant and my guess is Perez has greased more than one judge and DA in Albany law enforcement, plus its political machine. It's amazing what can go on when you turn a blind eye to crime and corruption for the sake of the almighty dollar.

As we pass by the massive brick building, I notice the three or four identical Suburbans parked outside on the street, plus two Range Rovers. A couple of gangsters are patrolling the area. They aren't openly carrying weapons, but I know they are concealing them under their shirts and muscle T-shirts. I also see one more vehicle. It's Sean's Volkswagen hatchback with the blown out rear window. Somehow, Don Juan must have driven it back here. Or someone did it for him. But it makes sense to me that he is avoiding a hospital to treat his wounds and his son's wounds for the same reason Joanne and I are. We will attract the police.

At least I know where Don Juan and what's left of his family will be residing for some time to come while they recuperate, and that's precisely why I'm taking the chance on making this drive-by. I also know something else: that's the place where Joanne's mother was brutally beheaded. But I say nothing about it. I also don't linger for too long just in case the gangsters spot one of their own SUVs making its way along Lark Street.

Driving on, I say, "Let's head to the hospital now."

Approaching the massive campus that is the Albany Medical Center, I pull onto a road marked DELIVERIES in bright red letters printed on a white sign. I take the road around the parking garage and that leads to the area behind the main hospital and physical plant. We pass by big tanks filled with CO2 and racks of piping attached to them, plus assorted smaller buildings, and maintenance sheds. When we come to a series of sliding glass doors marked MORGUE, I know we're in the right spot. A few feet away from the morgue entrance is a smaller sliding glass entry that reads, EMPLOYEES ENTRANCE.

I park just to the left of the morgue doors and get out, leaving the SUV running.

"Hang on," I say, inside the open door. "Be right back."

Heading into the morgue, I look around for a wheelchair. I realize that most everything that enters this space is going to be riding a mobile gurney, but medical centers are chuck full of wheelchairs, right? Still, nothing to be seen at first glance. I head down a dimly lit hall with an exposed ceiling. The place is eerily quiet with only the clanging of metal pipes and hissing from steam valves providing a somber soundtrack. Up ahead, I spot a waiting area that's got some chairs in it, a small couch, and a couple of end tables. A flat screen TV is broadcasting CNN, the volume silent. Located in the corner of the room are three folded wheelchairs. Bingo!

Pulling the first one out, I unfold it and begin wheeling it back towards the sliding glass doors. It's then I notice a couple of wood and glass doors situated just a little to my right as I exit the waiting area. Releasing my grip on the chair, I go to the doors, and carefully peek through the small chicken wire reinforced glass. The body set on one of the closest of half a dozen stainless steel tables makes me go dizzy. It's Esther. She's naked, other than two green sheets covering her private parts. Her head is placed where it belongs on a metal block, but there's maybe a four- or five-inch gap between her lower jaw and the neck to which it used to be attached. I've never seen a paler body. Not even Bradley Junior is that white and it makes me sick to my stomach to look at her empty of all her blood and her head detached from her body.

"I know we didn't get along very well, Esther," I whisper, "but God's speed."

Turning, I grab the wheelchair handles and exit the morgue as fast as humanly possible.

Wheeling the chair to the Suburban, Joanne opens the door, gets out.

"We'll have to do this together," she says. "He's deadweight."

"So long as he's not dead," I say.

Together, we gently slide him across the long back seat. Slipping my hands under his arms, I use all my leg and back strength to lift him by the shoulders and place him in the chair. Joanne slides his legs off the seat, and places them on the foot panels. Bradley Junior wakes up just slightly, issues a painful grunt, but then passes out again. I can't imagine the pain he is experiencing right now, so it's better that he's not conscious. But then, what the hell do I know? I'm just a simple mailman.

Taking hold of the wheelchair handles, I wheel our son the few feet to the Employee's entrance. I glance at my watch. If Jennifer is true to her word, she will be here in five minutes. I look around. Some hospital maintenance staff are coming and going from the maintenance sheds. They're not giving us a second look, which is a good thing. No one seems to be coming or going from the morgue. That's another good thing. For a split second, I consider telling Joanne about her deceased mother lying in state just a few feet away from us. But I'm not so sure she'd be able to deal with seeing her mom's body in that kind of mutilated condition, so I let it go.

"Let's get back in the Suburban," I say, "and wait."

We get in, and we watch the Employee's Entrance door like a pair of hawks. When it opens a couple of minutes later, and a small, attractive strawberry blond haired young woman dressed in green surgical scrubs appears, our collective hearts are lifted. Jill takes a quick look over both shoulders, and then simply walks behind Bradley Junior's wheelchair, and wheels him inside.

Glancing at Joanne, I can see the tears falling down her face. In a way, I guess I feel a little like crying too. It's true, we've saved our son from a madman. But in another way, we've saved him from ourselves, and from what we've become over these past three-plus months. Reaching out, I take hold of my wife's hand and squeeze it. I also lean into her and kiss her gently on her wet lips.

"Love you, Joanne," I say. "Always will."

"Love you more, honey," she says.

Pulling away from the morgue, I make for the exit. We've just one more item to check off our list before we can end this thing with Don Juan Perez.

15

What I'm about to do isn't going to be easy. But it's got to be done. We drive into North Albany, past Little's Lake and the Camp's old cabin, where we hook a left on the road that takes us to Hope Street. I take it slow while approaching my old neighborhood, just in case the police or FBI or both are patrolling the place. Making a left onto the street, I continue to go slow, while taking a long look at the yellow plastic crime scene ribbon that's draped over the front door. I can also spot the lockbox that's been placed on the door's opener.

Naturally, I don't stop at the house, but instead, drive maybe one hundred feet further into the neighborhood before parking in between two single-story ranch homes. It's going on late afternoon, but most people are still at work. But that doesn't mean I can take my time. I need to move fast if I'm about to get away with breaking into my own house without being spotted by one of my neighbors.

"What are we doing here, Bradley?" a still sad and still crying Joanne finally speaks up. "Isn't this a little reckless for us? Danish could show up at any time."

"I need something in the house, Jo," I say. "I will be back in just three minutes, I promise. I'll leave the engine running."

Before she has the chance to protest, I open the door, jump out, and make my way along an overgrown no man's land between two tall parallel wood fences that separate two individual backyards. I head for the same wooded property that separates my home from the Little's Lake state land. Bulling my way through the scrub and low hanging branches on the pine and oak trees, I come to my backyard. Like most of the backyards situated inside the Hope Street neighborhood, a big wood privacy fence surrounds it. Exiting the woods, I follow the fence around to the gate, open it, and enter the backyard. Jumping up onto the wood deck, I go to the sliding glass door. It's locked.

Here's what I know to be true: The house is unoccupied. There's also no alarm system installed since, until recently, I could never afford to have one installed. I also know this: Joanne and I will never be coming home to this house again. In fact, if all goes according to plan, Joanne and I will be in Mexico two or three days from now, max. I'm not entirely sure yet how I'm going to make it happen. All I know is I have the means to make it happen. The financial means, that is. We stay here, we go to prison for the rest of our lives and that is just not an option right now. It will never be an option.

All that said, I make my way to the outdoor table, grab one of the metal chairs, carry it with me back to the sliding glass door, and toss it through the plate glass. The glass shatters. I step into my home for the last time, head to my bedroom, go to the closet, grab my old postal worker uniform, including the lace-up shoes. I then take one more good look at the bedroom where we conceived our son, inhale and exhale a sad breath, and exit the house the same way I entered. Through the busted plate glass sliding door frame.

Heading back through the woods, to the fence line, I find the Suburban exactly the way I left it. The engine is still running, and Joanne is still sitting there, her facial expression tight and tense.

"I heard glass shattering," she says.

"That was our sliding glass door," I say, tossing the clothes on her lap. "I had to break in since I don't have a key to it."

"You might have tried the front door."

"It's got a police lockbox on it. No way I'm getting in that way."

I turn the wheel and make a U-turn. Joanne looks at the pile of clothes in her lap.

"If I knew you were grabbing a change of clothing, I would have asked you to grab me some clean undies."

"I'm sorry, Jo," I say. "I just wanted to get in and out."

"Did you at least grab the extra phone chargers? We left the others at the motel," she reminds me.

"Don't worry," I say. "We can buy a couple more. Let's just mail this package and get back on the road. The sooner we can get out of New York State, the better."

Turning out of Hope Street, we go back in the direction of the city. When the time comes, I turn onto the exit ramp for state highway 90, westbound.

"Where are you taking us now?" Joanne asks.

“We’re going to the post office,” I say. “I need to mail something, certified receipt request.”

She glances at her watch.

“It’s after four,” she says. “They’re closed.”

I turn to her and grin.

“I have the key to the back door.”

“What about security cameras?”

“I know this is hard to believe, but there’s no CCTV security,” I say. “None that’s operational anyway. This is a federally run outfit that loses billions per year. Security cameras are the least of their worry.”

She shoots me a quick look.

“I’m not sure I believe that,” she says.

“Not even most UPS outfits have CCTV cameras inside most of their warehouses and distribution facilities,” I stress. “Don’t believe me, look it up.”

“Okay I believe you.”

We drive some more until I arrive at New Karner Road, where I hook a left. I drive a few hundred feet until I come upon the employee’s entry road for the postal distribution center. Turning onto it, I come to a massive parking lot, which contains a whole bunch of vans, trucks, and even Jeeps, all painted white and boasting the USPS logo on their side panels.

Grabbing the clothing from my wife's lap, I go around to the back of the Suburban, open it, sit my butt on the carpeted floor, and proceed to pull my boots off. Stripping down to my boxers, I put on my old uniform, including the shoes. Turns out, the pants are so baggy I need to pull my belt out of the jeans and run it through the loops on my gray/blue trousers. The last time I wore this outfit, my belly spilled over the waist band. Joanne and I have truly changed. Physically, emotionally, legally. I shove the gun barrel into my pant waist.

Taking hold of my keys, I go to the passenger side window. Joanne rolls it down.

"I'll need you to get behind the wheel and be ready for me to exit the facility. Just in case there's a security guard on duty, we'll have to act fast."

"Thought you said they don't believe in security."

"Doesn't mean they don't believe in rent-a-cops. Remember when we killed Martin? Somebody had to have found him. That's why I'm wearing the old uniform. Case I run into somebody." Then, "I need your bag."

Reaching to the floor, she picks it up, sets it in her lap. I grab the plastic pipe.

"Be right back," I say.

"I'll be waiting by the employee's door by the back bays."

"Perfect," I say.

Walking toward my old place of employment, I feel myself working up a sly grin over what I'm about to do. Unlocking the employee entrance door, I head directly through the cavernous distribution center, past the massive steel conveyor belt that takes up the entire center of the four-story building like an indoor roller coaster, and finally through the double swinging doors and into the general post office. The plastic crime scene ribbon is gone, but there's a piece of plywood covering the now shattered glass entry. Setting the pipe on the counter, I grab a large cardboard envelope and open it. Rolling up some bubble wrap, I place it in the bottom of the package. Then I set the pipe inside, and stuff more bubble wrap on top of it.

Sealing the package, I go around the counter to Carol's computerized cash register. Pulling out a blank Return/Request/Receipt form, I pen in the name Don Juan Perez in the area indicated. I then add his Lark Street address, along with his cell phone number. Peeling back the slick backing, I stick the Return/Request/Receipt form to the package. As a final gesture, I stamp the package with priority overnight, first class delivery, which means Don Juan will not only receive the package first thing in the morning, but he will also be required to personally sign for it.

When that's done, I go into the back and dump the package into the outgoing mail bin.

"My work here is finished," I whisper, my grin growing even wider.

As I head back around the counter, I can't help but notice the new FBI poster that's been tacked to the wall. This one has real photos of Joanne and me. We look like we used to look in our previous lives. Joanne with her reading glasses on and her hair pulled back. A photo taken at the local library where she was volunteering. Me, dressed in my postal worker uniform, standing outside the open door to my truck on a hot summer's day, my face looking puffy, my soft beer gut sticking out. I'm smiling at the camera, but I don't know how happy I am. Like the song says, Joanne and I were older then. We're younger than that now.

Speaking of Joanne, if she's not already worried over where I am, she's soon about to be. Mailing the package has taken a few minutes longer than I expected. Heading back through the double swinging doors into the distribution center, I …

16

…The blow nailed me on the back of the head, and put me down on the spot. It also knocked me out, cold. I don't know how long I was out. One or two seconds, one or two minutes, one or two hours…it's not easy to tell. All I know now is my head hurts. Really…fucking…hurts. And when I reach for my gun, it's gone. As my eyesight begins to refocus, a man begins to take shape. He's standing just a few feet in front of me. He's not holding his service weapon on me, but my own 9mm semi-automatic. Rather, Sean's 9mm.

Detective David Danish.

He's smiling that same smile he wore on his smooth round face the morning he first stopped me in my minivan for a busted brake light back when he was still a uniformed traffic cop. Only now, he's wearing one of his blue suitcoats, a light gray button down, and a brown necktie. His tan trousers appear professionally pressed and his brown shoes are polished. Even his stand of short white hair looks perfect.

“Well, Mr. Jones,” he says after a time, “you sure have come a long way since being a postal worker. Or am I missing something here? By the looks of it, you’ve come back to real, honest work.”

Sitting up, I feel the back of my head. There’s no blood, but the lump that’s risen is already the size of an egg.

“Mind if I get up, Detective?” I say. “Or are you going to try to sucker punch me again?”

He laughs. “That wasn’t a sucker punch so much as a pistol whipping you never saw coming. It was also my way of taking control of the situation. You and your wife have become quite the Bonnie and Clyde these days. The body count you’ve left behind, the drugs you’ve cooked, the money you’ve laundered…my oh my.” He shakes his head slowly, like he’s also about to say Tsk, tsk, tsk. “You just might go down in the history books as one of Upstate New York’s most notorious crime teams. Congratulations. That’s quite the feat for two middle-aged people who drove a minivan and lived a sedate life of work, TV, bed for ages and ages.”

Slowly, I get myself back up on my feet. I’m a bit out of balance, but I’m confident I’m not about to fall back down again.

“Where’s this going, Danish?” I ask. “You gonna arrest me already, or what?”

He’s still aiming my weapon at me.

“That’s the thing,” he says. “To be honest, I had several chances to nab you already. But I’ve been holding back. When you killed the Camps, I was right behind you. When you killed your fellow mailman, Martin, I was close by. I was even there when your boy was gunned down in cold blood. Witnessed it with my own eyes. When you drove to Catskill to hide out, you never noticed me on your tail. But I was there, all the time." Pointing his extended index finger at me. "And let me ask you a question, Jones. Who disintegrates two grown men, buried what's left of their bodies in the basement, then tosses all the empty plastic acid containers, cement and lime bags in the recyclable waste can? Everybody knows cops always go through a suspect's trash."

Joanne would know that...

A slow burn emerges from my toes, up my legs, to my belly, past my beating heart and into my brain. It mixes with the adrenaline to form a red rage. I feel my hands forming fists. If only I had my own gun, I'd take my chances and pull it out. But then, I'm not sure I'm pissed off at him or me. I recall the few times I'd seen him drive past my house. Or seen him hanging around the Perez brother's crime scene, or even the Camp's crime scene. Now that I think about it, I do recall him driving past the same day my son got shot.

"So, the million-dollar question," I say. "Why didn't you arrest me when you had the chance? When you could have nailed me and Joanne red-handed?"

His smile grows wider.

"Let me ask you something else, Mr. Jones," he says. "How much did you make as a postal worker? Fifty, sixty K per year? Was that enough to put a roof over your head, send the kid to college and med school, plus keep your mother-in-law happy and cozy in her old age in a private elderly facility?"

For a long beat, I just stare at him, wondering what he's getting at.

"We never had enough money if you wanna know the truth," I say. "We were always in the red."

"And then, when your wife accidentally kills the two Perez brothers, and finds all those drugs and all that money just for the taking, you can't help yourselves. Not only that, you imagine the possibilities of entering a business where you can make not tens of millions, but hundreds of millions. And you know what? You'd reached an age where you were sick of the struggle. Sick of never getting ahead. Sick of seeing the neighbors get rich all around you, while you'd grown old, tired, and fat. How am I doing here?"

I'll be damned if he isn't right about everything. I nod.

"So, you get into the drug business thinking, what the hell. What could go wrong? Turns out your happy-go-lucky, drunk-as-a-skunk casket-selling neighbor, Sean, had been pushing drugs on the side for years and years for a nice Russian fellow by the name of Carcov, and nothing ever happened to him. For Sean, it was a matter of staying financially solvent. And isn't that what life comes down to? Staying financially solvent for your family? Never mind the kids or adults the drugs will hurt. The addicts are always going to find drugs no matter what. That's a cultural, political, and legal issue. You didn't invent it and it wasn't your idea. It's nothing personal when you sell drugs. It's just a case of supply meeting demand. A business no more deadly than selling booze or cigarettes."

Again, he's right and he knows it.

"So then, what about me?" he goes on. "How much money do I make? Do I have enough at the end of the month to make the private school tuition? The big house in the 'burbs? The wife's new Lexus? The country club she insisted we join? The weeklong trip to Turks and Kakos next month? The Macy's credit card, the Mastercard, the Discovery Card, the weekly donation to St. Pious Church? It's not all coming out of a cop's salary. Even a detective's salary. Maybe I make more than a mailman, but not much more. But you see, Mr. Jones, I want better for the wife and kids. I want what everybody wants. I want us to live the American Dream."

Now it's all becoming clear to me what he's getting at. He's not a cop, so much as he's me. Me *and* my wife.

"You want to live the American Dream," I say, after a time, "even if it means committing American crimes."

He smirks and laughs again.

"Hey, if you wanna put it that way," he says.

"Who's paying you, Danish? If you don't mind my asking. That's assuming I'm not walking out of here alive anyway."

"Jeeze, you gotta ask, Jones?" he says. "You didn't think Perez was going to let that performance you pulled off at King Fuels this afternoon go unanswered, did you? And let me tell you something: *Bravo!* You and the missus did some real Van Damage on those filthy gangbangers." He looks over both shoulders, as though someone out there is listening to us. He leans into me a little. "If you want to know the God's honest truth, you did us all a favor by getting rid of those bald headed, tattooed gangbanger creeps. They make me sick to my stomach." He glances at his watch. "It's getting late," he goes on. "I could chit chat with you all day. I like you, Jones. You *and* your wife. You've got balls you never knew you had. It's too bad it comes down to this, but you had to know deep down inside that once you got involved in the drug smuggling business, something like this was a real possibility."

My head is pounding, my stomach so tight it feels like it's about to split in two, my heart throbbing in my throat. In my head I picture Joanne. I picture Bradley. Will I ever see them again?

"I understand," I say through a dry mouth.

"Listen," he says, "I'll make it real quick. In the end, it will just look like you came back to this place to end your life. You couldn't take it anymore…the guilt, the shame, the sadness you caused so many people...so you returned to the one, pure place that was more sacred to you than church. The good old United States Postal Service where the people's mail gets delivered no matter what, by honest men and women in their gray postal uniforms. Get where I'm going with this, Jones?"

"I see the logic, Danish."

"Okay then, down on your knees, please."

I exhale, and suddenly take on this feeling of weighing twice my normal weight. Slowly, I drop to my knees, head down, chin against chest, hands resting on my head, fingers locked at the knuckles. I just want to get this the hell over with. The detective steps up to me, plants the pistol barrel against my right temple. In my mind, I picture what he's going to do when it's all over. He's going to wipe away his prints from it, and place it in my hand, wrap my finger around the trigger, just like Sean attempted with Mark Camp. Only difference is, Detective Danish won't fuck it up.

He presses the barrel tighter.

"By the way, Mr. Jones," he says. "I'm curious. What were you really doing back here in your old mailman uniform anyway?"

The shot reverberates through the distribution center. It also startles me enough to cause me to jump back up onto my feet while Danish drops to the floor, deadweight. I press my hand against my head. Is there a bullet in my brain and I just don't know it? But then I see my wife standing a few feet away, her short barreled semi-automatic gripped combat style in both her hands.

"Jesus, Jo," I say. "You scared the crap out of me. But goddamn I love you. You saved my life again."

"You owe me, Bradley," she says, her voice echoing in the big, wide open distribution center.

I gaze down at Danish. He's been shot in the lower back and the bullet has exited his upper right chest. There's a big round blood stain that's expanding on his expensive Oxford. He's also got a little blood exiting his mouth, like the bullet might have shattered and nicked his windpipe.

"What the hell happened?" he grunts, his eyes wide, his face turning pale.

Bending at the knees, I snatch my gun out of his hand before he shoots me with it.

"Somebody beat you to the draw, cowboy," I say. "That's what happened."

"You son of a bitch," he says, through his pain. "I should have shot you in the head the second I saw you."

"That's not nice," I say. "I thought you liked me, Danish."

“I’ll tell you what else is not nice, you lucky fucker,” the cop spits, “I hope you get caught and sent to prison for the rest of your sad lives.” He spits some blood. “And I hope your son dies. How’s about them apples?”

“Wow,” I say. “Some pretty harsh words for a dying on-the-take cop.”

“We’ll see who dies,” he grunts.

The blood stain from his chest wound is growing wider and wider.

“What do we do with him?” Joanne asks.

My eyes go from her to the conveyor belt and back again. An idea fills my head.

“Joanne,” I say. “Give me a hand.”

Like I did with my son earlier, I position myself behind Detective Danish. Bending at the knees, I slip my arms under both his arms and heft him up. He squeals in pain.

“Grab his legs,” I say, grunting.

“Where are we taking him?” Joanne asks, taking hold of his limp legs.

“The conveyor belt.”

Together we manage to place him on his back on the belt.

“What the fuck are you doing to me?” the cop begs, his fear as palpable as the blood leaking onto the wide black belt.

Mounted to the concrete block wall, near the double swinging doors, is a big green button. I go to it and punch it. An alarm sounds. That’s followed by a loud buzzer and then the sudden coming to life of the conveyor belt. A *loud* mechanical noise fills the giant distribution center as the belt starts running in the direction of the giant mail bins located in the adjoining building. When Detective Danish feels himself being carried away by the belt, he begins to panic and scream.

When he reaches the portion of the belt that's elevated at a thirty-five-degree angle, he starts heading upwards.

"No!" he screams. "Stop this now, Jones! Please stop it! Please…."

First, he disappears from view as he enters into the next building. Then we hear a shrill scream as the belt drops him two full stories into one of the empty bins below. A distinct thud follows and then nothing. Tomorrow, he'll be quite the sight for the mail sorters. If only I could see the looks on their faces when they come to his pale, stiff, wide-eyed body.

"Wait right here, Jo," I say.

I go to the wall, hit the red button that stops the conveyor belt. Then, heading further into the building, I enter the men's room, grab some paper towels from the dispenser and soak them in warm water. Exiting the bathroom, I rejoin Joanne. Dropping to one knee, I clean the relatively small amount of blood from off the floor. I'd look for the spent bullet, but we don't have the time for that. Anyway, when the postal workers discover the body in the morning, it will make any attempt at cleaning the place moot. It just seems like the right thing to do at the time. Making my way back to the bathroom, I flush the bloody paper towels.

When I come back out, I can't help but notice the sly smirk on Joanne's face.

"Did you really have to pull that conveyor belt stunt, Bradley?" she asks.

I cock my head over my shoulder, purse my lips. “I didn’t like what he said about our son.”

“I didn’t either,” she says.

“Follow me,” I say. “We need lodging for the night, and I think I know how to find it without attracting anymore police.”

Taking Joanne by the hand, I lead her through the swinging double doors and into the general post office.

17

My wife's hand gripped in mine, I drag her around the counter to Carol's computer. Typing in her first grandson's name, "Justin," plus the number "101 right after it in the password space (I've seen her enter this password dozens of times before), I then bring up the Google search engine, and type "Airbnb, Saratoga." A bunch of available places come up. Since we want something a little secluded, I narrow my search by typing, "Cabin." A couple dozen options appear.

"That one looks nice and cozy," Joanne says, pointing at a photo of a single-story cabin located in the middle of a lot surrounded by tall pines and oaks on all sides. The caption above it reads, "Secluded Weekend Getaway."

"It's not the weekend, but what the hell," I say, picking up Carol's phone and dialing the number provided.

The call is answered right away.

"Yes," says the voice of an old man. Or, an older man anyway.

“I’m inquiring about the cabin for rent on Airbnb,” I say. “Any chance it’s available tonight?”

“Little short notice, don’t you think?” he says.

“I know it is, and my apologies,” I say. “But I just got into town from a long business trip and my wife and I could really use a little seclusion, if you know what I mean.”

The man exhales, then laughs.

“Sure, I do,” he says. “I was young once. How would you like to pay?”

“PayPal?”

“Perfect,” he says.

He gives me his PayPal address, and I open another Google screen and bring up my PayPal account. I send him one hundred twenty dollars and wait.

“Got it,” he says. “How long till you get here?”

“Probably gonna take us about forty minutes or so,” I say.

“That’s my supper time,” he says. “So, what I’ll do is leave the key in the mailbox by the front door. You’ll find fresh towels in the bathroom and fresh sheets on the bed. Sure, I can trust you?”

“Is the Pope a South American Communist?” I say.

He laughs again.

“Good one,” he says. “Enjoy your stay and please don’t burn the joint down.”

“I’m a mailman,” I say. “You have my word.”

“Means I can trust you,” he says.

I hang up, and turn to my wife.

“It ain’t much,” I say, “but let’s head to the woods and get to know one another again, Jo.”

She’s not looking at me, but at the FBI Most Wanted poster.

“Ugh,” she says, “I hate that picture. I’m not nearly that old and chubby anymore.”

“Funny you should say that,” I add. “It’s exactly what I thought.”

Together, we haul our young criminal asses out of the Postal Distribution Center.

###

The Suburban has a full tank of gas. That’s our good luck. Our cell phones have no charge or chargers. That’s our bad luck. But on the way up north, I pull off the New York Route 87 highway and enter the quiet town of Malta and hit up the first Verizon store I can find in one of the dozen or so strip malls that line the boulevard.

“Maybe you should do the honors on this one, Jo,” I say. “I seem to have bad luck with stores lately. And you have an innocent looking, pretty face.”

“Why thank you, Bradley,” she says. “It’s about time you noticed.”

She reaches into her bag, pulls out yet another stash of cash, peels off a couple Benjamins, stuffs them in her jeans pocket.

“Be right out,” she says.

While she's gone, I turn on the radio, listen for the news at the top of the six o'clock hour.

"…while Detective Danish is not considered a missing person yet," says the female reporter, "Albany police officials are beginning to worry. It should also be noted that the body of Esther Gleason, the mother of suspected drug runner and murderer, Joanne Jones, showed up mysteriously at the Albany Medical Center morgue. Thus far, no workers at the Anne Lee Home for the Aged and Infirmed, where Gleason lived, have given any indication that they witnessed the eighty-eight-year-old woman being forcibly removed from the facility. Nor have any workers at the Albany Medical Center morgue taken responsibility for receiving the body, all of which is leading authorities to speculate that hush money payoffs were made by either the Perez organization or a rival cartel family.

"On a good note, the physician son of suspected drug runner/murderer, Bradley Jones, was apparently dropped off at the Albany Medical Center, perhaps by the same person or persons who dropped off Joanne Jones's deceased mother, although this is pure speculation at this point. One thing is for certain, however, the Jones Gang, as they are now known, are nowhere to be found in the greater Capital District area, and it is further speculated by both the Albany Police Department and the FBI, that they have already fled the city.

"Reporting for Spectrum twenty-four hours news, this is--"

I kill the news as Joanne exits the store with a plastic Verizon bag in hand and a curious smile painting her face. Opening the door, she gets in. I pull around the parking lot and take a left onto the road that will bring us back to the highway.

"Why the smile, Jo?"

“The kid who waited on me…an Indian kid as in India…thought I looked like someone famous, but he couldn’t put his finger on it. So, eventually, he said he knew me from the TV. He asked me if I was Jennifer Anniston.”

I gaze at her out the corner of my eye as I make a right onto the on-ramp and punch the gas.

“You gotta be kidding me,” I say.

“No joke,” she says.

I pull out into light traffic.

“So, what did you say?”

“I told him, ‘You never know.’ He gave me my change and I left.”

I place my hand on her thigh.

“Who knows,” I say, “I just might get lucky tonight with Jennifer Anniston.”

Minutes later we hit up a small, mom and pop grocery store after we get off the highway for a second time at the Saratoga exit and head into the countryside towards the rural town of Greenville. This time we both take the chance of entering the store since it looks, from the outside anyway, that no security cameras have been installed. Once we’re inside, we can see there’s no television set anywhere in sight either. Of course, people tend to look at their phone these days for most of their news, so that doesn’t mean we won’t be spotted. But my gut instinct tells me, we won’t be. After all, maybe Joanne and I have gotten ourselves back into excellent physical shape over the past few months, but we’re still just a simple middle-aged couple. A retired postal worker married to a housewife and part-time library volunteer.

We grab ourselves a couple steaks, some salad fixings, some bread, and of course, beer. We also grab some bottled water and for the morning, coffee, orange juice, and a half carton of eggs. Bringing it all up to the counter, a girl of maybe fourteen rings us out. She's listening to the pop music that's blasting through her earbuds while she bags the food. She doesn't say a word since she's living in another world altogether, but she does offer a nice smile as we pay cash, and she quickly makes the correct change. It's a silly thought, but as we exit the store, I realize this is the last time I will shop for food in New York State.

We drive another ten minutes into deep country. Joanne has her phone plugged into the SUV charger so she's able to find specific directions to the place via GPS.

"Turn here," she says as we approach a two-track with a nearly hidden road sign that reads, "Highlands Road. Private"

"Turn your phone off now," I say.

"On it," Joanne says, powering down her phone but keeping it plugged in to the charger. "The FBI can track our position if we're not careful."

"Netflix," I say.

She smiles. "Yup, thank God for Netflix."

I turn onto the road. We feel the bumpiness of the ride as we head deeper and deeper into the forest. When we come upon a clearing, we find the cabin. I pull up near the front door, kill the SUV engine.

"Home sweet home," I say. "For a night anyway."

"We're pretty well hidden up here," Joanne says.

“Let’s get this food inside and lock the door,” I say. “I’m dying for a beer.”

“Think I’ll join you.”

Grabbing the key out of the exterior wall-mounted mailbox, I unlock the door. The cabin interior isn’t much to look at. A stone fireplace is located to the right as you enter through the front door, and an old brown leather couch is pushed up against the pine wood wall to the left. A small galley kitchen is situated to our direct right and to our direct left, is a small bathroom with a shower stall. The opposite wall contains a picture window which looks out onto the forest and what I imagine are the mountains in the distance. But since it’s night, you can’t see anything. A round kitchen table has been placed against the big window wall.

We both step into the kitchen, drop the bags onto the wood block counter beside the stove. On the opposite side of the fireplace is a small bedroom. It’s got a double bed that has a quilt on it, and four pillows. Joanne goes to the double-hung window and opens it.

“That’s better,” she says. “Stuffy in here.”

That’s when I place both my hands on her shoulders. Spinning her around, I kiss her on the mouth, hard. Throwing her down on the bed, I then undress her while she tries to undress me. It’s all very clumsy but wonderful. It feels just like it did when we were back in college, and everything was new again.

When we’re naked, we don’t bother with getting under the covers. I enter her right then and there, our mouths never disconnecting. My heart pounds against her heart and for a time it’s like we’re one in the same person. Everything is building up inside me and I feel it building up inside her too, and it doesn’t take long for us both to reach that special place. We both release explosively, and when it’s finally over, we roll onto our backs.

Joanne places her head on my chest. When she wipes her eyes with the back of her hand, I know she's crying.

"I'm so sorry, Bradley," she says.

I shush her. "It's okay, baby." I run my hand through her hair.

"I'd rather die than drift from you again," she says, sniffling. "Do you believe me?"

"Even Bonnie and Clyde made mistakes sometimes."

"Bonnie and Clyde" she says. Then, "Do you regret what we've done? If you had to do it all over again, would you?"

I take a moment to think about it.

"Some people died because of us," I say. "Including your mom. We nearly lost Bradley. But you wanna know something, Jo?"

"I'm listening."

"If we die tomorrow, we can truly say that for a very short time, we really lived our lives. We lived on the edge, and we took chances almost no one takes and, in the process, we've never felt more alive in all our days. At least, that's how *I* feel about it."

She turns to me then and kisses me on the mouth with her wet lips.

"You are so right, Clyde," she says. "And I love you with all my heart."

"Right back attcha, Bonnie," I say. "Now, how about a cold beer."

We drink a few beers in bed, and we laugh even though there isn't a whole lot to laugh about considering our crimes. But sometimes, you gotta look on the bright side. After a time, I send a text to Jill's phone (yes, I remember her number), and she in turn sends us a selfie of she and a much healthier, much happier, Brad Jr., sitting up in bed. He's heavily bandaged and no doubt sedated, but otherwise bright eyed and giving us the thumbs up, while she is smiling and sitting by his bedside, looking beautiful, young, and full of real love. Who knows, maybe sooner than later they will marry and bring us some very beautiful grandchildren.

There's not much more to speak of that night, other than we make an incredible steak dinner which we eat in bed. We drink a couple more beers apiece and then fall asleep in each other's arms to the fresh country air. No Netflix tonight. Instead, we sleep the sleep of the dead, only we're alive and lucky to be so.

When early morning arrives along with a brilliant sun, we make some eggs, drink some coffee, clean the kitchen, and head back out on the road. Soon we'll be on our way to the Mexican border. But not quite yet. Maybe he doesn't know it yet, but Don Juan Perez is about to get one last visit from his old partners in the Bubble Gum business.

18

It's ten AM by the time we re-enter the Albany city limits. As opposed to last night, Joanne has tensed up again. I can see it on her face the closer we come to Lark Street and the Perez inner city brick fortress.

"This visit to Perez," she says. "I suppose it has something to do with that contraption you sent him."

"That it does," I say. "And you've watched enough crime shows and read enough crime novels to know precisely what that contraption is, don't you, Jo?"

She turns to me, nods.

"I know what it is," she says. Then, inhaling and exhaling. "This will be the Don's demise if it works. It's possible that the Russian boss, Carcov will be there, plus the three men who worked for us." A second heavy inhale and exhale. "What you…what *we*…are about to do…it's all okay with me, so long as no innocents are killed in the process."

"Don't worry," I say, turning onto Lark Street. "This isn't the 2012 Boston bombing which was an evil act by evil people. I've thought it all out, weighed the risks." Glancing at my watch. "Don Juan will have gotten his mail by now. He will have signed for the package. I can only assume he is alone in his office or perhaps his son is with him, while they both recuperate."

Driving along Lark Street, we come upon the big brick, street corner mansion. Unlike the previous day, the morning has turned cloudy, breezy, and cool, like Fall is finally coming in fast. There's also the look and smell of rain in the air. I head past the street corner mansion, and park along the curb maybe one hundred feet up from it. A few SUVs are parked outside the mansion against the curb.

I also notice another vehicle. It's the long, black, Fitzgerald funeral home hearse. It tells me Karl/Lurch and his two cohorts, Skinny Jay and Smirking Jack are inside the basement, cooking a fresh batch of Bubble Gum. Like Joanne said, maybe Carcov is with them. I can just see the tall, blonde-haired Russian, dressed in his blue track suit, his vodka/beer gut protruding from it like a nine-month pregnancy. He'll be observing the action while standing in the back of the cooking room, safe enough away from the cooker's fumes. Or perhaps he'll be seated at a table, counting the cold hard cash that's arriving inside the MacDonald/Jones caskets.

I see no innocent pedestrians walking past the place. Only gangbangers occupy the exterior in their baggy jeans and wife beater T-shirts. Even on a good day, I can't imagine innocent passersby taking a chance on walking on that side of the street. They will instead cross the road to the other side.

Reaching into Joanne's bag, I pull out the walkie talkie/homemade remote detonator. I turn it on. Static fills the SUV.

“I don’t know if I can watch this,” Joanne says. “But then, I can’t keep my eyes off it either.”

It’s not necessary for me to aim the remote device in the direction of the house, but I shift myself around in my seat, and do it anyway. Tuning onto the correct radio frequency, I place my thumb on the transmit button.

“This is it, Joanne,” I say. “This is the end of our war with Don Juan Perez. This is when the Jones’s from Hope Street in North Albany win the day!”

“Wait,” she says, reaching out. “Let me.”

I feel my stomach tighten up.

“You sure?”

“The man shot our son. He had every intention of killing our boy. He decapitated my mother, for God’s sakes.” She pauses for a breath. “Yeah, Brad, I’m real sure.”

Carefully, I hand her the remote detonator.

“Just press the transmit button,” I say. “That’s all it takes.”

She’s seated in the passenger side seat, her back to the building, a strange smile painting her face.

“This is for mom, Don Juan,” she says. “And this is for Bradley, Junior.”

She presses the transmit button.

19

A Year and One Half Later

Tulum, Mexico

The day is bright and because of the ocean breeze, not overly hot, even for Tulum in June. The spot the kids chose for their wedding day couldn't be more perfect if it was chosen by the good Lord himself. It's a smallish affair for a Mexican wedding with maybe seventy white wood folding chairs set up on the groom's side and an equal amount on the bride's side. Not only is every single chair occupied, but some folks are standing in the back—the women in their pretty skirts and dresses, the men in sharp suits, and some in tuxedos.

The wood, stage-like platform where the vows are about to be recited has been painted virgin white and draped with hundreds of white roses. It is positioned almost precariously on the edge of a small cliff that overlooks the deep blue ocean. The smell of the sea is in the air, and so is love. Love and harmony.

Joanne sits beside me in the first row, her hand holding mine tightly. While I'm wearing a custom-tailored black tux, she's wearing a bone-colored cocktail dress adorned with sequins. It cost sixteen thousand dollars and had to be shipped from New York City by special private carrier. No U.S. post office down here. Her privately trained body looks ravishing in the dress and her long dark hair is lush and perfect. She no longer wears thick eyeglasses now that she's had Lasik surgery from the man who's considered the best eye surgeon in all of Mexico. If you were to meet her for the first time, you would swear Joanne isn't the mother of the groom, but instead his sister. Okay, maybe an older sister, but certainly not his mother.

The black-vested Latin priest approaches the handsome couple as they take their positions on the platform, Bradley Junior is clean shaven, big, tall, handsome and happy as I've ever seen him. And Jill, dressed in her white satin gown, her hair pulled up in a bun, her stunning face looking as if it were carved from the best Italian marble and just as delicate, is a beautiful apparition to behold. Her striking blue eyes blanket my heart and soul with warmth.

"Do you, Bradley, take this woman to be your lawfully wedded wife?" the priest asks.

"I do," Bradley says.

Joanne squeezes my hand even harder and begins to cry.

"Do you, Jill, take this man to be your lawfully wedded husband?"

"I do."

"I now pronounce you man and wife," the priest says. "Mr. Dr. Jones, you may kiss your bride, Mrs. Dr. Jones."

That's when the crowd breaks out in laughter. It's a very funny quip for a priest who seems to take his job very seriously. Even Joanne laughs through her tears. My son takes Jill in his arms and plants the sweetest kiss on her you ever did see. My own eyes well up as the entire place explodes in applause. That's also when my mind begins to spin, and the events of nearly two years unfold in my head. From the moment Joanne pressed the transmit button on the remote detonator, to the explosion that shook the city and at the same time, took out the entire Perez fortress and everyone inside it, including Don Juan, and his sole surviving son. An estimated thirty-five gangsters were also killed in the blast, plus our three former funeral home employees. No word about a man identified as a Russian national named Carcov was ever mentioned in the reports, but that doesn't mean he also didn't buy the farm in the explosion.

Technically speaking, the blast from the pipe bomb itself was *not* enough to take out the entire four-story brick and cement structure. But it was powerful enough to trigger the explosive fumes coming from the basement cooking setup, turning what was intended to be a small explosion into a massive, chain reaction blast that was said to shatter the windows on many buildings that flank Lark Street.

We calmly drove out of the city that morning, and hit the highway southbound, neither one of us saying a single word for over an hour. And even then, we spoke in short, muted sentences. It was as if we were in shock, not at the blast, so much as what we'd accomplished in the few short months since we'd become drug runners involved in a drug war with a Mexican cartel leader, and how much we'd changed in the process.

We drove through the day and into the night, careful to keep our phones off, only stopping for gas and for food. By the end of the second day, we were in Nevada, and by the next morning, we were in San Diego. By then, the shock had worn off, and it was a matter of getting across the border which, it turns out, wasn't hard or dangerous at all, thanks to Joanne and Sean, God rest his beer-soaked soul.

It had been around the time we reached Nebraska on the second day that it became apparent we'd need new identities, plus all the documents required to go with them. But how would we manage to get the necessary materials made in just twenty-four hours while we were on the run? It was just a matter of contacting one of Sean's friends. Not to bring up painful memories but having gotten closer to Sean than I would have preferred, Joanne's brief affair with him did turn out to be a bit fortuitous considering she'd met some friends of his that could help us out. She even had one of them in her speed-dial. A man named Morris who, like Sean worked in both the casket and the drug business and who had a friend who knew a friend who knew a friend who, for a price, could help us out with everything we needed.

That said, by the time we reached the California border, Morris not only arranged for us to pick up our new identities at a pre-disclosed commercial mailbox location, but we were also given specific direction on when to cross into Mexico via the San Diego/Tijuana border. We were even instructed as to which lane to drive in, and how to respond to the specific questions the border guard would be asking us. We were to ditch all weapons and make sure our cash was stored on our person. The SUV was to be as clean as a whistle and I was to stop at a hardware store for a glass repair kit to fix the two bullet holes in the center of the windshield—a project that turned out to be *easy peasy, lemon squeezy* as Joanne was fond of saying now and again in our old, boring, broke life.

For all this, we were instructed to PayPal Morris two hundred fifty thousand dollars. No negotiation. No refunds. I didn't argue with him one bit. I paid the man right away and, as a result, we didn't just make it across the border into Mexico unscathed and unmolested by both U.S. ICE officials and Mexican border patrol, we positively skated in.

Of course, there was no way we were going to make it to Sean's funeral, much less Joanne's mother's funeral. Something that saddened Joanne to no end, but then, what choice did she have? As for me, I was still disgusted at the brutal method Don Juan Perez chose to end Esther's life. But then, on the inside, I couldn't help but be reminded of something Sean used to say, especially on a Sunday afternoon in the Fall, when we were watching football and getting drunk on Budweiser cans in his basement man cave. Sunday evenings were almost always reserved for having dinner with Esther who would spend much of her time berating me to no end, not only for my lack of ambition, but for my three decades-plus inability to keep Joanne in the luxury she'd grown accustomed to when growing up.

He'd say, "Bradley buddy, I know you and your mother-in-law butt heads, and that's putting it lightly. But you gotta keep in mind something that used to crack up ole' Winston Churchill about a telegram a buddy of his received regarding the death of his mother-in-law. 'How shall we proceed?' asked the sender of the telegram. Churchill's buddy telegraphed back, 'Embalm, cremate, bury at sea. Take no chances.'" Sean would crack up and slap me on the back with that one. Even now, after everything we went through together, I can't help but smile when I think of it.

Speaking of funerals, Don Juan's and his son's double memorial service made national, if not international news. It was also attended by just about the entire Albany Democratic Machine, including the DA and the Mayor. Detective Danish never made it out of the Post Office alive. Curiously, his death hasn't been pinned on Joanne and me since little if no physical evidence of our presence was found on the scene. He was however, buried with full police honors, regardless of his special business relationship with Don Juan Perez.

###

We weren't in Tulum all that long setting up house along a wide stretch of white sandy beach, when one morning a couple black Suburban's like the one Perez loaned me (that's a joke) pulled into our wrap-around driveway. Several big, suited men in sunglasses with two-way radio devices inserted in their ears, emerged from the second SUV, while a third suited man emerged from behind the wheel of the first SUV.

The man riding shotgun was not wearing a suit, but instead, jeans, flipflops, and a colorful red and yellow flowered Hawaiian guayabera shirt. His hair was long and thick, and it was also more gray than dark. His beard and mustache matched it perfectly. I pegged him for maybe sixty-four or five but going on forty. A man who seemed to enjoy life and all it had to offer and who refused to grow up. He was wearing RayBan aviators and, while at first, I had my guard up, he approached me with the sweetest smile you ever did see.

"Mr. Bradley Jones, I presume?" he said, a friendly hand outstretched before me. "I am Don Pedro Escobar, Pablo's big brother. I was wondering if you happened to have any Bubble Gum on you?"

What followed were some beers and tequila shots on the veranda that overlooked the ocean and some beautiful, young topless sunbathers. Joanne joined us for a couple of rounds. She found Don Pedro to be quite charming and funny. I have to admit, he was quick with a joke. The short of it was that he offered us a partnership deal. If we could somehow replicate the Bubble Gum recipe, he would pay us handsomely for our efforts. If we decided against working with him, no worries, we could live out our days not only in peace, but he would see to it that we were protected by his own personal security service. After all, we'd done the Escobar cartel a great service. Something that took me a little by surprise. And as he was leaving, I couldn't help but ask him something that weighed heavily on my mind.

"Don Pedro," I said, "something isn't making sense to me."

"What is it, amigo?"

"Don Juan Perez became my enemy. We went to war against one another. Some people even blame his death on me and my wife."

Don Pedro stole a few moments to chew on that.

Then he said, "What you pulled off against a ruthless killer like Don Juan is nothing short of miraculous. From what I'm told, you were a simple postman before getting into the business, and your wife, a simple woman of the house. You were fading into middle age, obscurity, debt, and before you knew it, death. Until you took out Perez's little brothers and, in the process, somehow gained his trust. You also created an amazing product which made us millions upon millions and can potentially make us so much more. Escucha, Mr. Jones, what happened between you and Don Juan is not your fault. You did what you had to do to protect you and your family. You should not be shot for it. You should not be skinned alive or beheaded. On the contrary, you should be commended and offered the opportunity to make tens more, if not hundreds of millions more dollars. Not for you and the lovely Joanne, amigo. But for your big family to be. Your child, your grandchildren, and their grandchildren. Do you believe me?"

I didn't know what it was about Don Pedro, but he possessed something that made me trust him. The feeling in my gut was the exact opposite of when I first met Don Juan and all the ugly, violent gangsters that surrounded him with their shaved heads and their horrid tattoos. To put it mildly, he was offering Joanne and me the chance not of a lifetime, but many lifetimes.

"My wife and I will give your offer a lot of thought, Don Pedro," I said. "It might take a little leg work on our part to retrieve the precise recipe. But it can be done. In any case, we have been honored to have you in our home as our special guest."

"I look forward to hearing from you soon, Mr. Jones," he said.

He smiled warmly as he turned and walked into the golden sunset.

That was many months ago now, and as it turns out, the small home we purchased on the ocean was sold for a much larger hacienda. No scratch that, more like an oceanfront estate. How did we manage it? It didn't take Joanne long to decide if we should get back into the Bubble Gum business with Don Pedro. Like me she had a good feeling about him. She was also quite confident that she could replicate the recipe by once again contacting her friend Morris, who, you guessed it, knew a friend, who knew a friend, who knew a friend, all of whom had been working associates with you guessed it, the late Sean MacDonald.

Thus far, our Bubble Gum sales have not been limited to the northeast region of the US but the globe over. Just like Don Pedro promised, we have made not tens of millions in profit, but hundreds of millions. We do it all under the guise of having begun a lucrative Mexican import/export business. We've even established the equivalent of a limited liability organization with the Mexican government. It's been quite the ride for a retired postal worker, and former part-time library volunteer.

Now, watching my son embrace his lovely new wife, my heart is filled with joy. I have my family. I have a new life with my wife and best friend, Joanne. I have money to be passed on to generations of Jones' to come. Soon, I will have my first grandchild. What more could a middle-aged man want?

When the applause dies down, the now freshly married Bradley Junior and Jill step off the platform and make their triumphant walk down the center aisle to more claps and cheers from their adoring family and friends. Photos are snapped and video filmed with smartphones. The videographer we hired from straight out of Hollywood is following them along with a crew that contains professional sound and lighting people. My son's videotaped wedding will be nothing less than a Hollywood production.

Moments later, both families of the bride and groom line up shoulder to shoulder. Since Joanne and I are the hosts for this great event, she and I take our place first in line, she standing to my right-hand side. The first person to greet us with a handshake for me, a gentle kiss on the cheek for Joanne, and hearty congratulations all around, is none other than Don Pedro Escobar himself. He's wearing an expensive sport coat over pressed jeans and lizard skin cowboy boots. As always, he's wearing his RayBan aviators. He not only shakes my hand, but bear hugs me also.

Bringing his lips to my ears, he whispers, "I have something important to tell you. You are no longer simply Mr. Jones, Bradley," he says. "From now on, you are to be known as something else. Something more befitting of a man of your importance and prestige." His focus shifting to Joanne. "The same will go for your lovely wife also."

That's when he does something incredible. Reaching into his jacket, he pulls out a gold ring, which he places on the third finger of my left hand. Taking Joanne's hand in his, he places an identical ring on the same finger on her left hand. It's the same finger we wear our wedding rings on.

Don Pedro then drops to one knee. Once again, he takes my hand in his, kisses the ring. He takes Joanne's hand in his, and kisses her ring.

Slowly standing, he says, "It is my great honor to be the first to address you both as Don Bradley Jones and Dona Joanne Jones. May your lives be long and healthy."

And that is how the Jones' are resurrected, saved from what was a sure death by boredom, complacency, ill health, and financial ruin. In a word, the death of the American Dream. But we were born again into something we never could have imagined not that long ago.

Now, as I inhale the fresh sea air, what I must ask myself is this: What's wrong with this picture? There's not a damn thing wrong with it. I'm standing beside my beautiful wife on a cliffside that overlooks the ocean and a property that contains my big white mansion and several other large homes that will be occupied by my children, and my grandchildren. We are richer than God, we are healthy and happy, and have a wonderful future ahead of us. It is a life many men and women can only dream about.

Therefore, what I should be asking is this: What's *right* with this picture?

Maybe the Lord works in mysterious ways, but sometimes fate can be more mysterious. Whatever the case, this is not the end of our story. It is instead, the beginning. A beautiful beginning for two people who were once old before their time, but who are now happier and younger than ever before.

Let the dancing begin.

THE END

If you enjoyed BOOK IV of American Crime Story, please read all the episodic American Crime Story Books in order. Just go to www.vinzandri.com to get them all.

Winner of the 2015 PWA Shamus Award and the 2015 ITW Thriller Award for Best Original Paperback Novel for MOONLIGHT WEEPS, Vincent Zandri is the NEW YORK TIMES and USA TODAY bestselling author of more than 160 novels and novellas including THE REMAINS, THE EMBALMER, THE SHROUD KEY and MOONLIGHT WEEPS. He was also a finalist for the 2019 Derringer Award for Best Novelette. Zandri's list of domestic publishers includes Delacorte, Dell, Down & Out Books, Thomas & Mercer, Polis Books, Blackstone Audio, and Suspense Publishing. An MFA in Writing graduate of Vermont College, Zandri's work is translated in the Dutch, Russian, French, Italian, Japanese, and Polish. He was the subject of a major feature by the New York Times in 2015 and he's also made appearances on Bloomberg TV and FOX news. In December 2014, Suspense Magazine named Zandri's, THE SHROUD KEY, as one of the "Best Books of 2014." Suspense Magazine also selected WHEN SHADOWS COME as one of the "Best Books of 2016." A freelance photojournalist and the author of the popular YouTube podcast, The Writer's Life, Zandri has written for Living Ready Magazine, RT, New York Newsday, Hudson Valley Magazine, Writers Digest, The Times Union (Albany),

Game & Fish Magazine, The Jerusalem Post, Strategy Magazine, and many more. He lives in Albany, New York and Florence, Italy. For more go to WWW.VINZANDRI.COM

Bear Media/Bear Noir 2023

http://www.vinzandri.com

Author Photo by Jessica Painter

Published in the United States of America

The author is represented by Chip MacGregor of MacGregor Literary

Milton Keynes UK
Ingram Content Group UK Ltd.
UKHW050801041223
433752UK00015B/747